Girl TALK

Best Friends

Have you seen all the
Best Friends
books?

Spotlight on SUNITA

Narinder Dhami

BBC

First published in 1998 by BBC Worldwide Ltd
Woodlands, 80 Wood Lane, London W12 0TT

Text by Narinder Dhami copyright © BBC Worldwide Ltd 1998
The author asserts the moral right to be identified as the
author of the work.

Girl Talk copyright © BBC Worldwide Ltd 1995

ISBN 0 563 40552 X

Cover photography by Jamie Hughes

Thanks to Empire

Printed and bound by Mickays of Chatham plc

Let **Girl** TALK introduce you to the greatest bunch of Best Friends ever...

First there's

along with

She's entered her dream comp **Sunita**

Anya but can they both make it?

a lesson in football! **Lauren**

Best Friends

They're supported by

Gemma

unlike

who's busy giving **Cara**

who's got little sister trouble

Chapter 1

"Girls playing football!" sniffed Sunita's grandmother disapprovingly, as she bustled round the living-room, duster and polish in hand. "I can't understand why any girl would want to play such a terrible, rough game!"

"I'm with you on that one, Gran," Sunita said with a grin. "But Lauren loves it, and she's really good at it too."

Mrs Banerjee sniffed again. "I'm surprised her parents allow it." She frowned at her granddaughter. "Maybe it's better if you don't go, Sunny. You can stay here and help me clean the house."

Sunita looked alarmed. Even standing around in the cold watching a boring football match was better than dusting and polishing!

Spotlight on Sunita

"Oh please *Dadima*," she begged, trying to persuade her gran by using her favourite pet name. "I promised Lauren I'd go. The manager of the district team is coming to watch the match, and Lauren's hoping to get chosen for their next game. It's really important to her."

"Oh, all right," Mrs Banerjee said grudgingly. "But I *really* don't approve of girls playing football."

"I'm only going to watch Lauren, Gran," Sunita pointed out patiently. "I'm not planning on rolling around in the mud myself!"

Mrs Banerjee looked shocked. "I should hope not!"

"Although Lauren *did* say that the team was short of a player or two," Sunita went on wickedly. "Maybe they'll ask me to fill in!"

Mrs Banerjee fixed her granddaughter with a beady stare, then marched huffily out of the room.

Sunita couldn't help laughing. She could just imagine the fireworks in the Banerjee household if she turned up one day in a football strip! Her gran didn't always approve of some of the things Sunita and her friends got up to, and she particularly didn't approve of Sunita's burning ambition to be a fashion designer when she grew up. Sunita's parents weren't happy about it either – Mr

Banerjee wanted his daughter to become an accountant.

"But I'd be the only accountant in the world who's hopeless at maths!" Sunita had wailed during one of their many 'discussions' on the subject.

"Then you'll just have to work harder at your sums," her gran had chimed in, and Sunita's parents had nodded in agreement. But Sunita had no intention of adding up numbers for the rest of her life. She was determined to follow her dream, even if it meant going against her family's wishes.

It wasn't easy, though. Sunita's parents hadn't actually forbidden her to draw, but if they saw her with her sketchpad and pens, they always managed to find her something else to do, and Gran was particularly good at keeping her busy. But this afternoon Sunita knew that everyone except her older brothers Ganesh and Vikram would be out, so she would have plenty of time for her designs. She was really looking forward to it.

'Actually, it's a shame I've got to go to Lauren's football match this morning,' Sunita thought with a sigh, 'I might've been able to sneak upstairs and do a bit of sketching while Mum and Gran are cleaning the house.'

But she knew she couldn't let her friend down –

she had to be there to support her. Lauren was so excited at the prospect of playing for the district team, she hadn't stopped going on about it since she'd told the girls last Sunday. Sunita remembered back to that afternoon round Lauren's house...

"The manager's coming to watch our team play next week!" Lauren bounced up and down madly on the sofa, ham sandwich in hand, scattering the crumbs everywhere. "She'll be looking for girls to play for the district team, so I've really got to impress her!"

"But you already play for a football team," Carli had said, looking puzzled and pushing her glasses up her nose.

"Oh, that's just the stupid little sports centre league!" Lauren declared impatiently. "The district team's *cool*! They travel to matches all over the county."

"Well, I reckon the district team'll snap you up!" Gemma said, as she handed round a plate of chocolate eclairs. Gemma and Lauren had been best mates for years, and Gemma knew how much sport meant to her friend.

"I hope so!" Lauren looked round at her friends.

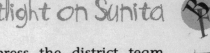
"And I'm going to impress the district team manager even more with my own special fan club there to cheer me on!"

"Who's that?" Carli asked.

"You lot, of course!"

The girls stared at Lauren in amazement, and Anya nearly choked on her eclair.

"You mean you want us to come and watch you play?" Sunita asked, trying hard not to sound too dismayed. Lauren might be crazy about football, but she was the only one who was.

"Yep!"

"Will you be playing on the indoor pitch?" Gemma asked hopefully.

Lauren shook her head. "No, we're outside this week. You don't mind, do you?"

"Mind!" Anya wailed, finally getting over her coughing fit. "Of course we mind! Look!" She gestured dramatically at the rain beating against the window. "You don't seriously think we're going to stand around getting soaked to the skin while you mess about with a stupid ball? We'll get pneumonia!"

"Oh, don't be such a wimp!" Lauren said cheerfully. "It's still nearly a week to the match. The weather's bound to get better."

Anya wasn't convinced. "Oh yeah? Who says?"

Spotlight on Sunita

"I do!" Lauren pulled a cross-eyed face at her. "Anyway, a bit of rain won't kill you!"

"Can't you get your dad to fix it so your team can play inside?" Gemma asked. Lauren's father worked at the sports centre as facilities manager, and often gave the girls free passes for the swimming pool.

"No, I can't," Lauren said indignantly. "There are loads of teams playing this weekend, and we have to take it in turns to use the indoor pitch. Look, I need some support if I'm going to impress the district team manager. You'll all come, won't you?"

"Yeah, sure!" Gemma said immediately. Sunita and Carli looked at each other and also nodded heroically. Anya, who hated being left out, still hesitated.

"Oh, all right," she muttered at last, picking up the remains of her eclair. "But don't be surprised if I end up with a streaming cold!"

Sunita grinned to herself as she remembered the disgruntled look on Anya's face. Still, at least it wasn't raining today, she thought, glancing out of the window. But it was cold, and the sky looked grey and dismal. It wouldn't be much of a surprise if Anya suddenly went down with instant chickenpox or a sprained ankle, and didn't turn up at all.

Sunita checked her watch. Mrs Standish had promised to pick her up at a quarter to nine, and it was already ten to. Not that Sunita was surprised. The Standish household was a manic one, and the family hardly ever made it anywhere on time. Idly she picked up the remote control. It was Saturday morning, so almost all the TV channels were showing children's programmes, and every time she flipped the switch, yet another cartoon came up. Sunita wasn't interested in any of them, but as she flicked through, one of the cartoons finished.

"Welcome back to *Live on Saturday*," said a good-looking, dark-haired young man. "Hope you enjoyed the cartoon. And now here's Eva with some news about our very special competition..."

The camera moved to Eva Jones. She was small and slim with long blonde hair, and she was sitting on a large purple sofa.

"Thank you, Kit," she said with a smile. "Yes,

these are just some of the entries for our 'Young Fashion Designer of the Year' competition, which we told you about last week." She waved a hand at two bulging mailbags. "And, as you can see, we've had hundreds of designs sent in…"

Sunita wasn't listening. She was busy thinking about the drawings she was going to work on that afternoon. She'd had an idea in her head for ages for a short black and white dress with big buttons and complicated sleeves that she was dying to get down on paper…

Then she blinked. Just a minute… Had she heard the words 'Young Fashion Designer of the Year' or hadn't she? Quickly she turned the volume up.

"…If you were watching last week, you'll know that what we want you to do is design an outfit you think will look good on *me*," Eva went on. "And we've had some fabulous designs sent in already…"

Sunita's eyes lit up. This was the opportunity she had been waiting for – a chance to show exactly what she could do! But the competition was already up and running – how much time did she have left to come up with an entry?

"Well, those are just some of the drawings we've received." Eva Jones put the sheets of paper down, and turned back to the camera. "But if you think you can do better, send in your own sketches."

"Yes!" Sunita squealed. She flew across the room and grabbed a pen and some paper as the address flashed up on the screen. Her heart pounding with excitement, she quickly scribbled it down. The Banerjees' doorbell rang right at that moment, but Sunita was in another world and didn't even hear it.

"And remember," Eva went on, "you've only got until Tuesday to get your entries in, so you'd better make it fast!"

Sunita gasped. Tuesday? That was only four days away. That meant she would have to post her design by Monday afternoon at the latest. That left only three days – no, two-and-a-half, really, because she wouldn't be able to make a start until this afternoon. Could she do it?

"We'll be announcing the three finalists in five weeks' time," Eva was saying. "They'll be invited on to the programme, and their outfits will be made up and modelled by yours truly."

The cameras cut back to Kit, who was standing next to an expensive-looking computer. "Our first-prize winner will receive not only this state-of-the-art PC, but also the chance to spend a day at Elena Moreno's studio!" He grinned. "And don't forget that Elena herself will be one of our judges."

Spotlight on Sunita

Sunita was thrilled to bits. Elena Moreno was a young British designer, and her clothes were worn by pop stars, film stars and princesses. Meeting Elena would be a dream come true, Sunita thought excitedly. But first she had to win the competition...

"Sunny, what's the matter with you?" Her gran hurried into the living-room, looking annoyed. "Your friends arrived five minutes ago. Didn't you hear the doorbell?"

"No, Gran. Sorry." Sunita turned the TV off and jumped to her feet, quickly tucking the piece of paper holding the competition address into the pocket of her jeans. She knew that her gran wouldn't approve of her entering the competition, and neither would her parents, but that wasn't going to put her off.

Sunita was determined to have a go, even if she had to do it in secret...

Chapter 2

Sunita hurried down the hallway. Lauren was on the doorstep, hopping impatiently from one foot to the other.

"Hurry up!" she yelled. "I'm going to be late!"

"Sorry," Sunita gasped. She was about to tell Lauren about the Young Fashion Designer of the Year competition but she didn't get a chance. Lauren hustled her out of the house – while Sunita was still trying to get her jacket on – and down the path to the car, where the others were waiting.

"Hello, Mrs Standish," Sunita said breathlessly. "Hi, everyone."

"Hello, Sunita," said Lauren's mum. "Jump in."

Gemma moved closer to Anya on the back seat, so that Sunita could get in.

"Where's Carli?' asked Sunita as she helped

Gemma put on the middle seatbelt.

"Her mum's walking her there," explained Anya with a yawn. "They'll probably be frozen solid before they arrive!"

Gemma rolled her eyes, and Sunita smiled. "What about the rest of your family, Lauren?" she asked.

"Dad's working," Lauren replied, buckling herself into the passenger seat. "But he's going to try to come and watch my match. Ben's team are playing away, and Gemma's mum's looking after Harry."

"That's lucky," Sunita remarked, just managing to shut the door, "or we wouldn't all have fitted in the car!"

"Mind my new boots!" Anya said sharply, as Sunita shifted around, trying to get comfortable.

"Sorry," Sunita said with a grin as she saw the sulky look on Anya's face. "What's up with you, anyway? I thought you'd be glad it isn't raining."

"Why?" Anya snapped. "I won't get wet now, I'll just freeze to death instead!"

"Oh, get over it!" Lauren snorted as Mrs Standish revved up the old Ford Escort and drove off. "You haven't stopped moaning since we picked you up."

"Well, I told you I didn't want to come," Anya muttered sullenly.

Lauren twisted round in her seat, looking hurt. "Well, I'm so sorry for thinking you might actually want to come and support one of your best friends! I thought you were part of this gang."

Anya looked shocked. "I am!"

"No, don't worry about it." With a haughty look, Lauren turned away and folded her arms. "If that's how you feel, my mum will run you straight back home, after she's dropped us off at the match."

"I was only joking, Lauren," Anya said quickly. "I'm really looking forward to watching you play. Honestly."

"Really?" Lauren raised her eyebrows.

"I said so, didn't I?"

"Try sounding as though you mean it!" Lauren retorted.

"I think you'd better stop winding Anya up, Lauren," said her mum. "And by the way, I'm not your taxi driver – *I'll* decide when to drop Anya home!"

"Oh, that's all right, Mrs Standish." Anya declared enthusiastically, going completely over the top as usual. "I'll be cheering the loudest, you wait and see!"

"You're very quiet, Gemma," Mrs Standish remarked as Lauren and Sunita tried not to laugh at Anya's exaggerated enthusiasm. "Are you all right?"

Spotlight on Sunita

Sunita suddenly realised that Gemma hadn't said anything since she'd got into the car. In fact, for the last five minutes she'd been staring out of the window. Sunita wondered what had happened. It took a lot to get Gemma upset.

"I'm fine, Mrs Standish," Gemma mumbled, but Sunita could see at a glance that she wasn't. She looked pale and worried.

"What's up, Gems?" she asked her friend in a low voice. But Gemma glanced at Mrs Standish, and shook her head.

"Tell you later," she mouthed. Sunita nodded.

"I've got something to tell you too," she whispered back. She was dying to tell the others about the competition, but she couldn't risk saying anything in front of Mrs Standish, in case it got back to her parents. But right now she was more worried about Gemma.

"Right, here we are." Mrs Standish pulled into the car park. "Lauren, I..."

But Lauren was already out of the car and racing towards the doors of the sports centre.

"Got to go!" she yelled. "I'll find Dad on my way to the changing-rooms and tell him we've arrived!"

"That girl's got more energy than the electricity board!" Mrs Standish sighed, shaking her head.

14

"Can we get a drink in the café before the game?" Anya asked hopefully as they all climbed out of the car.

"No time, I'm afraid." Mrs Standish glanced at her watch. "We'd better go and find a place on the touchline. Look! There's Carli, waving her mum off."

Mrs Standish led them over to Carli, who gave them a big grin in welcome.

Gradually, more and more spectators arrived, ready for the match to begin. Anya shivered and pulled her coat around her more closely. "How long do football matches last anyway?" she said under her breath to Sunita.

"About three hours," Sunita said solemnly.

"*What*?" Anya wailed. Sunita managed to keep a straight face for about two seconds before she and Carli cracked up. Even Gemma managed a smile.

"Oh, very funny!" Anya tossed her dark hair back angrily, almost losing her fur hat in the process. "You didn't fool me one bit."

"It's usually ninety minutes," Carli said between giggles.

"Oh, ha, ha," Anya snorted. "No, come on, what is it really?"

Carli stared at her. "It *is* ninety minutes. Forty-five minutes in each half."

Anya turned pale.

"*Ninety minutes?*" she squealed, horrified. "You mean we have to hang around in the freezing cold for *ninety minutes?*"

"And a fifteen minute interval," Carli added.

"But that's – that's – ages!"

"Don't worry, Anya." Sunita could hardly speak for laughing. "They don't play such long games in the junior league. It'll be a lot shorter than that."

"Five minutes would be long enough for me," Anya muttered, fishing in the pockets of her jacket for her matching gloves.

The outdoor pitches were at the back of the sports centre. There were four of them, and all but one had boys' matches in progress. There weren't many people watching any of these games – at least compared to the crowds now waiting for the girls' game to start. Sunita nudged Gemma.

"Looks like all the girls have had the same idea as Lauren!" she murmured.

Gemma nodded. "We'll have to make sure we shout louder than everyone else," she said.

After a few minutes of nothing happening, Anya began to stamp her feet theatrically and blow on her fingers, a look of intense suffering on her face.

"What *are* you doing?" Sunita asked. "You're acting like we're in the North Pole or something!"

Mrs Standish cut in before Anya could reply. "I'm just going to have a word with Tania's mum," she said, waving at a blonde-haired woman who was standing across the pitch. "I shan't be a minute, girls." Tania James was in the girls' class at school, and was also a member of the football team.

"This is ruining my new boots," Anya complained as Mrs Standish left. "My heels keep on sinking right down into the mud."

"Never mind, keep still and everyone will just think you're wearing flat boots," Carli said, straight-faced. Sunita and Gemma both started laughing, and even Anya, who looked shocked because Carli was usually so quiet, managed a smile.

"You're looking a bit brighter, Gems," said Sunita, glancing at her friend. "Are you all right?"

Gemma's face clouded again. "Not really," she muttered. "I've had another row with Lucy."

"What, again?" said Anya. It seemed Gemma and her sister were always at each other's throats these days. "I thought your mum grounded you last Saturday because you guys had a fight."

"She did." Gemma kicked miserably at a clump of grass. "And now I'm not getting any pocket-money this week. Mum says she's had enough."

"What happened?" Carli asked.

Gemma shrugged. "She lost one of my CDs this

17

morning, that's why we had a row."

"Poor Gems," Sunita said sympathetically. "I'd go mad if one of my brothers did that to me."

Gemma blushed. "I did. I thumped her, and then she pulled my hair, so I guess that makes us even. But Mum went ballistic."

"I'm glad *I* haven't got any brothers or sisters," Anya said, pulling first one foot and then the other out of the mud. "My half-brothers are bad enough!"

"Thanks, Anya, that was a great help." Sunita glared at her. "Can't you see Gemma's upset?"

"Brothers and sisters aren't so bad," Carli said quietly. "Well, I don't know about brothers because I haven't got any, but my Annie's all right."

Gemma turned to Carli. "Don't you and Annie argue?"

"'Course we do, all the time," Carli said cheerfully. "But I don't let it get me down too much. I just try and ignore her!"

"Well, I *can't* ignore Lucy," Gemma muttered. "I hate her. I wish I was an only child."

Sunita and Carli gasped, and even Anya looked surprised.

"Wow, Lucy must've *really* got to you, Gems," said Sunita. "That's not like you."

Gemma looked ashamed of herself. "I know...

It's just that ever since Mum started working at the supermarket, she gets tired, and she wants me to look after Lucy all the time. It's always 'Gemma, take Lucy to the park' or 'Gemma, go and play with your sister', and it's driving me crazy!"

"Maybe you should have a word with your mum about it," Carli suggested.

"Maybe…" Gemma made an effort to cheer up a bit, and turned to Sunita. "You said in the car that you had something to tell us, didn't you?"

For a second Sunita didn't know what Gemma was talking about, and then, with a jolt of excitement, she remembered. Of course! The competition.

"That's great!" Gemma said eagerly when Sunita had explained. "I think you're in with a brilliant chance of winning!"

"So do I," Carli added. Carli was excellent at drawing herself, but she specialised in cartoons. She'd seen some of Sunita's fashion designs and thought they were amazing.

"Young Fashion Designer of the Year," Anya said thoughtfully. "I think I'll enter that myself!"

"But you can't –" Gemma stopped herself just in time from saying that Anya couldn't draw to save her life. "Well… er… I suppose you *have* got a lot of clothes!"

"Yes, I have!" Anya preened herself, then nearly keeled over as her heels stuck fast in the mud. The other three collapsed into giggles again as she just managed to keep herself upright by clutching at Lauren's father, who'd come over to join them.

"Hello, girls," Mr Standish said as he set Anya upright again. He was a well built, dark-haired man who seemed to live in tracksuits and trainers. "I hope you four are going to shout your heads off for our Lauren."

"Oh, we will, Mr Standish," Gemma promised, and the others nodded.

"Did you see Lauren?" Sunita asked. "How is she?"

"Nervous," Mr Standish replied with a grin. "But, you know Lauren. Once she starts playing, she'll forget about everything else."

"Is the district team manager here?" Carli asked.

Mr Standish nodded. "That's her over there," he said under his breath. "The woman in the black coat. Her name's Suzanne. Suzanne Thornton."

They all had a sneaky look. Suzanne, tall and dark-haired, was standing on her own near one of the goalposts, notebook in hand.

"Really?" Anya said. "She looks too pretty to be interested in football."

Sunita and Gemma both rolled their eyes, but before they could say anything, a huge cheer went up from the crowd as the players ran out onto the field.

"Here they are!" Gemma said. "COME ON, LAUREN!"

"COME ON, LAUREN!" the others joined in. They were all determined to yell the place down if it would help Lauren to get a place in the district team...

"GOAL!"

Cheers went up from the crowd, as Lauren kicked the ball as hard as she could. It flew into the back of the net like a bullet, whizzing past the opposition's goalkeeper.

"Yes!" Lauren yelled, overjoyed. The match was almost over, and her team had been losing 1-0 for the last half an hour. Now the scores were level.

The rest of the team rushed up to Lauren, and began slapping her on the back, but they didn't have much time to celebrate. A few seconds later, the referee's whistle blew to signal the end of the game.

"Hey, that was close!" Lauren panted to Tania

Spotlight on Sunita

James, as they shook hands with the opposing team. "We nearly didn't make it!"

"Mmm." Tania, who was a bit of an airhead despite her ball skills, was too busy patting her blonde curls back into shape to take much notice. "I wonder what the district team manager thought."

Lauren suddenly remembered that Suzanne Thornton had been watching the match. She'd seen the woman with her notepad straight away, standing by one of the goalposts when the teams first ran out, but then, as the game got underway, Lauren had forgotten all about her. Now, there was no sign of her.

Lauren felt bitterly disappointed. Surely Suzanne would have hung around to speak to her if she was impressed? Obviously, then, the manager wasn't interested in her for the district team...

"Well done, love!" Mrs Standish gave her daughter a big hug as she came off the pitch. "You were great!"

"Yes, you were brill!" Gemma added.

"Great goal!" Sunita and Carli said together, and even Anya looked impressed.

"Thanks." Lauren had to swallow a large lump in her throat before she could ask the question, "But what happened to Suzanne?"

"Oh, she had to leave before the match ended," Mr Standish replied with a huge grin. Lauren couldn't understand why her father was smiling, nor why everyone else was grinning at her too.

"So she didn't see my goal, then," she said gloomily.

Mr Standish shook his head. "No, she didn't. But she came over to talk to me before she left…"

Lauren's eyes widened. "What – what did she say?" she gulped.

"Oh, just that she was very impressed with a certain striker called Miss Lauren Standish." Mr Standish beamed at her. "She didn't promise anything, but I wouldn't be surprised if you're invited for a trial with the district team sometime very soon!"

"YES!" Lauren screeched at the top of her voice. She flung her arms round her dad, and then turned a couple of cartwheels across the grass. "I did it!"

"Now get yourself off to the changing-rooms before you catch your death of cold," Mrs Standish ordered her. "You won't be any use to the district team if you've got double pneumonia!"

"I've got to get back to work," Mr Standish said, glancing at his watch. "See you later, girls."

Lauren turned to grin at the others as her dad hurried off.

"Isn't it brilliant?" she said happily as they walked over to the changing-rooms. "I'm going to be in the district team!"

"You're not in it yet," Anya pointed out, and Lauren pulled a face.

"I will be!" she said confidently, throwing a mud-stained arm round Anya's shoulders. "You'll have to come and see me play my first district match!"

The other girls giggled as Anya's face fell.

"Oh – er – I'll look forward to it!" she said heroically.

"Sunita's got some news too," said Carli.

Lauren looked interested. "Oh? What?"

Sunita glanced over her shoulder to check that Mrs Standish was out of earshot. Lauren's mum was a little way behind them, talking to Mrs James again.

"I'm going to enter the Young Fashion Designer of the Year competition!" she said breathlessly, and quickly filled Lauren in on all the details.

"Of *course* you'll win!" Lauren said immediately. "Your designs are cool!"

"I've got to come up with an idea first," Sunita pointed out, but she couldn't help feeling encouraged by the support of her friends.

"Oh, you will!" Lauren declared enthusiastically.

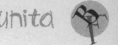
"I'm going to be in the district team, and you're going to win that competition – you'll see!"

Gemma laughed. "Maybe Sunita could create a special strip just for you!"

"Yeah, I can see it now!" Lauren put one hand on her hip and pretended to be strutting down a catwalk "And here is Sunita Banerjee's latest design, modelled by the famous footballer, Lauren Standish – a bright pink shirt and shorts, trimmed with gold sequins and silver lace!"

The girls fell about laughing.

"Somehow I don't think *that* would win the competition!" Sunita remarked.

"Never mind, you'll think of something!" Lauren linked little fingers with Sunita, and the other girls quickly linked up with each other as they whispered their special motto.

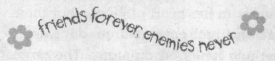

friends forever, enemies never

Sunita glowed with happiness inside. The confidence her friends had in her work really inspired her, and she couldn't wait to begin trying out some ideas for the competition.

Chapter 3

Sunita reached for her sketchpad and pens. She lay down on her bed and began flipping through the pages, looking at the designs she'd been working on for the last few weeks, wondering if there was something there good enough to send in as her competition entry. But she knew in her heart of hearts that there wasn't. What she really wanted to do was to create something new and dramatic. The problem was finding the time to do just that.

She hadn't managed even to start work on her designs after the match yesterday. Sunita's aunt had phoned unexpectedly to say that she and her family would be visiting them on Sunday afternoon, and Sunita's mum and gran had immediately cancelled their plans to go shopping, to start a marathon round of cooking and baking for their guests. Sunita, of course, had been roped in to help too.

Meanwhile, every hour was bringing the competition deadline on Tuesday closer and closer. If she didn't get started soon, she wouldn't have a design ready to post tomorrow – and then her chances of winning the competition would be over.

Sunita had gone up to her room after breakfast, telling her gran that she was doing homework. She felt guilty about the fib, but she told herself that she'd never get her design done otherwise...

"Sunita!" her mum called up the stairs. "Gemma's on the phone for you."

Sunita sighed. She shoved her sketchpad under the duvet, and went downstairs.

"Hi, Sunita!" Gemma sounded a bit brighter this morning. "I was wondering if you wanted to come round to my house. Carli's here already, and Anya and Lauren are going to come round really soon."

"Oh, sorry, Gems, I can't." Sunita glanced nervously down the hall to the kitchen where her mum and her gran were, and lowered her voice. "I'm going to try to do some work on my drawing this morning."

"Oh, right," said Gemma, understanding at once. "Well, if you change your mind, just give me a ring."

"Sunny, don't be too long on the phone."

Sunita's grandmother bustled out of the kitchen, wiping her floury hands on a towel. "Hurry up and finish your homework, and then you can come and help your mother and me."

"But, Gran, I was thinking of going over to Gemma's," Sunita said quickly, her mind working at lightning speed. "We've got some really hard maths homework to do, and Gemma's going to help me."

Mrs Banerjee hesitated. "All right," she said, "I'm glad to see that you're trying to improve your maths, Sunny. But you must be back by lunch time."

Sunita let out a sigh of relief as her gran went upstairs, and then turned back to the phone.

"Did you hear that?" she asked Gemma in a low voice.

"Yeah, I did." Gemma was laughing. "You don't *really* want to do maths homework, do you?"

"Don't be an idiot!" Sunita grinned. "I was wondering if I could work on my design at your house? I might get a bit of peace and quiet there!"

"'Course you can! See you in ten minutes."

"Make that five!" Sunita said, and she dashed upstairs to get her sketchpad and pens.

"Come on, Thumper." Gemma picked the rabbit

up, and put him back in his hutch. "You've had your run around. Now it's Snowball's turn."

"Hello, Snowball!" Carli waited until Thumper was safely locked away before letting her white rabbit out. She kept Snowball at Gemma's house because pets weren't allowed in the council flats where she lived. Gemma's father had built a large wooden hutch for Snowball, which sat next to Thumper's. "She's getting bigger, isn't she!"

"Yep, she'll soon be big enough to have babies," Gemma said, stroking the rabbit's soft fur. "Then we can put her and Thumper in the same hutch!"

Carli's eyes lit up. "That'll be *brilliant*! How long did the vet say we had to wait before Snowball's old enough to be a mum?"

"About three weeks," Gemma replied. She loved animals, and wanted to be a vet herself when she grew up. "Then it takes about four weeks for the kittens to be born."

"I thought only cats had kittens!" exclaimed Carli, looking puzzled.

"Baby rabbits are called kittens, too."

"I see," said Carli. "And it really only takes *four* weeks?"

Gemma smiled and nodded.

Snowball was now lolloping down towards the bottom of the garden, where Lucy and Annie were sitting in the greenhouse, playing with their Barbie dolls. Gemma was relieved that Carli had brought her sister with her this morning – Annie would keep Lucy out of her hair for a while.

Carli noticed Gemma suddenly looking gloomy, and touched her friend's arm. "What's up, Gems?"

Gemma shrugged. "Oh, the usual. I had a fight with Lucy yesterday, when we got back from Lauren's match. Luckily, Mum was talking to Mrs Standish at the time, so she didn't find out."

"What did you row about?"

Gemma thought for a moment. "I can't even remember!" she sighed. "But you know I wanted to spend Saturday afternoons helping out at the animal sanctuary where we got Snowball?"

Carli nodded.

"Well, Mum says she hasn't got time to take me there because she has to work most Saturday afternoons during the next couple of months," Gemma went on miserably. "And that means that me and the brat have to go to the garage with Dad, if Mrs Standish can't look after us."

"That must be pretty boring."

"Tell me about it!" Gemma shook her head despairingly. "Dad makes me and Lucy sit in the office, and all we do is fight!"

"Have you always argued a lot?"

Gemma thought about it. "Yeah, pretty much!" She managed a smile. "But it's definitely got worse since Mum started work. Lucy knows I'm fed up with looking after her all the time, and she just tries to wind me up!"

"Maybe she's jealous of you," Carli suggested.

"Jealous!" Gemma's eyes opened wide. "Why would Lucy be jealous of *me*?"

"Well, because you're clever, and you're good at so many things," Carli stammered, blushing pink with embarrassment. "You're ace at maths, and science, and you're kind, and you've got loads of friends... Maybe Lucy wants to be just like you."

Gemma was shaking her head, also looking embarrassed. "I don't think it's anything like that," she muttered. "Lucy is Mum's pet. Mum always takes her side."

"Then maybe Lucy is just as fed up with your mum working."

Before Gemma could say anything, the back gate opened, and Anya rushed into the garden. "Hi, girls!" she called, breathlessly. "Just wait till you see what I've got!"

"Another new outfit, by the look of it," Gemma said with a smile. Anya was wearing black jeans and a fluffy pink jumper they hadn't seen before.

"Oh, this old thing." Anya shrugged. "No, have

a look at this!"

She pulled a piece of paper from the pocket of her jeans, and held it out. "My dad took me shopping yesterday, and he bought me a CD-ROM – 'Top Fashion Designer'," Anya explained smugly. "It's excellent!"

Gemma and Carli looked at each other. The sketch of a girl in an orange and black dress was beautifully presented, but they hadn't got the heart to tell Anya that her design was actually quite dull. It had none of the flair and originality that was so obvious in Sunita's drawings.

"It's lovely, Anya," Carli said quickly.

Anya smiled broadly.

"But if you've already got a computer," Carli continued, "why are you bothering to enter?"

Anya's grin went wonky as she tried to think of a good answer to the question. "Well, I want to swap tips with Elena Moreno!" she blustered. "Anyway, what about Sunita? Has she done anything yet?"

"She's up in my bedroom, working on it now," Gemma replied. "She couldn't get any peace at home."

"Hi, you lot!" Lauren waved at them over the garden gate, and then came in. She was in tracksuit and trainers, and had a football tucked under her arm. "Want to help me practise for the district team trials?"

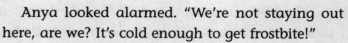

Anya looked alarmed. "We're not staying out here, are we? It's cold enough to get frostbite!"

"Wimp!" Lauren yelled, slinging the ball at Anya. Anya tried to catch it but missed, and the ball bounced off down the garden. Annie and Lucy came out of the greenhouse to see what was going on.

"Come on, Anya!" Lauren called. "Kick it back to me!"

"Can we play? Can we play?" Lucy shouted excitedly. She looked very much like her older sister, except that her hair was a slightly darker shade of brown, and her eyes a paler blue.

"I thought you two were playing your own game," Gemma sighed. "Go on, buzz off. We don't want little kids hanging around."

Lucy folded her arms and glared at her sister. "We want to play football!"

"I don't," Annie muttered anxiously. She was a small, slightly-built child who took life very seriously, and didn't like arguments. "Let's go and get a drink, Luce."

Lucy hesitated, her small, round face turning pink with anger. Then she nodded. Gemma heaved a sigh of relief, as the two little girls walked off towards the kitchen.

"Thank goodness!" she said. "Come on, then, Lauren, what do you want us to do?"

Spotlight on Sunita

"I need to practise my shots," Lauren replied, picking up the ball. "Anya, you can be goalie."

"Goalie!" Anya said, outraged. "If you think I'm flinging myself down on the muddy grass, you can think again, Lauren Standish!"

Lauren ignored her, and sent the ball flying in her direction. Anya jumped quickly aside, and let it bounce into a nearby flower-bed.

"You're supposed to catch it, Anya, not get out of the way!" Lauren roared crossly, chasing after it as Sunita came outside.

"What's up with Lucy and Annie?" she asked. "They've got their heads together like they're plotting something!"

"Oh, never mind them!" Gemma said. "Have you finished your design?"

Sunita shook her head miserably. "I haven't even started!"

"Have a look at mine," Anya said eagerly, pulling the piece of paper from her pocket.

Sunita took the drawing, and studied it. While the dress was nothing special, there was no doubt that the drawing was beautifully presented, and might just catch the judges' eye. Her heart sank even further.

"I haven't got *any* ideas," Sunita muttered, gloomily. "And time's running out. I don't think I'm going to be able to enter the competition after all…"

Chapter 4

"Sunny! Where have you been?" asked Mrs Banerjee as she ushered Sunita into the house. "Auntie Kamini and her family are here, and everyone is asking about you."

"Sorry," Sunita said, pulling off her jacket. She had stayed at Gemma's house longer than she should have done, trying to find some inspiration for her design. But the more she'd thought about it, the more her mind had refused to come up with a single good idea. Now they had visitors, and tomorrow there was school. Even if she did manage to come up with something, would she even have time to work on it? Sunita felt frustrated and unhappy, torn between the conflicting demands of her family and her own hopes and dreams.

The Banerjees' living-room was packed with people. Sunita's gran was handing out cups of tea, and Mr Banerjee was passing round plates of samosas, bhajis and pakoras. Sunita's brothers, Ganesh and Vikram, were squashed onto the sofa, talking gloomily to their Uncle Rajesh, who was quizzing them about their school work.

"Ah, here's Sunita." Auntie Kamini, a tall woman, elegant in a pink and gold sari, smiled as her niece came into the room. "We thought you'd got lost!"

Sunita forced herself to smile, as she was hugged and kissed by all the women in the room. They were all relations, some aunts, some cousins, some second cousins, and even Sunita wasn't quite sure who was who. She squeezed on to the sofa between Auntie Kamini and her mum, and fixed a bright smile on to her face while she answered questions about her school. All of the women were dressed up in their best visiting clothes, and the blaze of colours, of red, pink, blue, orange, green, purple and gold, in the Banerjees' living-room was like an enormous, glittering rainbow...

Of course! Sunita suddenly had such a brilliant idea that she almost jumped up and shouted it out at the top of her voice. The glowing colours of the women's saris and their *shalwar kameez*, the intricate embroidery and floating fabrics had given her a wonderful starting-point for her competition entry. She would design an East-meets-West outfit, a stunning trouser-suit a bit like a *shalwar kameez* but with the shirt a little shorter, the trousers a little less baggy... something that women of either culture could wear and look cool in.

"Sunny?" Sunita gradually became aware that her mother was frowning at her. "Are you all right?"

"Yes, I'm fine," Sunita said breathlessly. Now that she had an idea, she could hardly wait to get started. But would she have time to finish it by tomorrow?

Of course she would, Sunita told herself determinedly. She had a torch – and that meant she could work under her duvet after she was supposed to be asleep tonight. One way or another, she was going to get this design finished, and post it tomorrow afternoon...

"NOT ANOTHER WORD!" shouted Mrs Gordon, slamming a couple of burnt slices of toast down onto the plate in front of her. "I'm fed up with the pair of you!"

Spotlight on Sunita

"But, Mum, *she* started it!" Gemma yelled over the sound of the doorbell ringing.

"Didn't!" Lucy roared, kicking the table leg.

"Did!"

"*Didn't!*"

"*Did!*"

"Well, *I'm* finishing it!" Mrs Gordon declared furiously, as the doorbell chimed yet again. "That'll be Lauren – I'm supposed to be doing the school run this morning, and look how late we are!" She stomped across the kitchen to throw the toast into the bin. "I don't want to hear another sound from either of you! Now get your things, and let's go!"

Gemma waited until her mum had gone to get her coat, then she glared at Lucy. "I've told you before, brat! *Don't* go into my bedroom without permission!"

Lucy pouted. "I only wanted to borrow a pen!"

"You took my best felt-tips!" Gemma snapped. "Just keep out, or I'll bin your teddy bear. You'll never see him again!"

"Mum!" Lucy wailed, but Mrs Gordon simply covered her ears as she came back into the kitchen.

"I don't want to know," she said firmly, handing the girls their lunchboxes. "Now, I'm sorry your lunches aren't very exciting this morning. All the crisps seem to have gone over the weekend, along with that pack of Kit-Kats I bought. I think that father of yours is developing a sweet tooth in his old age!"

The doorbell rang once more, and they all hurried out of the house. Lauren was waiting for them on the doorstep.

"At last!" she said. "I was beginning to think you were still in bed!"

"Not quite," said Mrs Gordon grimly. "Having World War Three would be more like it." She unlocked the car. "Lucy, you sit in the front with me. I don't want you and Gemma arguing again."

"Oh, *Mum*..." Gemma began, but Lauren took charge of the situation, and bundled her friend into the back of the car.

Sunita was standing on the Banerjees' doorstep, looking out for them. As soon as she saw the Gordons' car, she bolted down the path and dived inside.

"Sorry, we're late, Sunita," Mrs Gordon apologised as she pulled away.

"How did you get on?" Gemma whispered. "Did you come up with anything?"

Sunita nodded as she fastened her seatbelt. "Show you later," she whispered back.

"What are you saying?" Lucy whined, craning

her neck round to find out what was going on.

"Shut up, you pain!" Gemma snapped. "It's none of your business!"

Mrs Gordon sighed as she pulled up outside Lucy's school. "Whatever happened to sisterly love? Bye-bye, sweetie. Be good."

Lucy jumped out of the car and hurried into the playground, where Annie was already waiting for her, and Mrs Gordon drove on to Duston Middle School, where she dropped off the others.

The minute her mum had gone, Gemma turned eagerly to Sunita. "Come on, let's see your drawing, then!"

"Let's find Carli first," Sunita said. "She'll want to see it as well."

Carli was waiting for them in the playground, and they all went off into a quiet corner. Sunita pulled a large brown envelope from her schoolbag, and took out the piece of paper inside.

"Oh, Sunita, it's gorgeous!" Gemma gasped.

"It's lovely," Carli added, her eyes wide behind the thick lenses of her glasses.

Even Lauren, who wasn't really into clothes, was impressed. "It's great, Sunita," she said admiringly. "You're going to knock the judges' eyes out!"

Sunita had designed a beautiful outfit in silky

cream and gold material. The suit, a short top and slim-fitting trousers with slits at the ankles, had a matching, flowing cream scarf, scattered with tiny gold stars. She'd created an outfit that was striking and fashionable without being over the top.

"It isn't finished yet," Sunita said, putting the envelope back in her bag. "I've got to try and get it done today, so I can post it after school, otherwise I'll miss the closing date."

Gemma frowned. "That only gives you break and lunchtime. D'you think you'll do it?"

"I'm going to have to work on it in lessons," Sunita said, a determined look on her face.

Lauren whistled. "That's a bit dodgy, isn't it?" she asked. "What if Ms Drury catches you?"

Sunita shrugged. "I'll just have to risk it."

"Let's hope Ms Drury's having one of her dozy days," Gemma said hopefully, as the bell rang and they headed into the school building. "Then we could stage a fashion show in class, and she wouldn't even notice!"

Ms Drury was Class 6's form teacher. While she was popular with the girls, she did sometimes seem to be on another planet. Today she was wandering around the room handing out their English books, looking even more dippy than usual, her long red hair swept up into an untidy ponytail.

Spotlight on Sunita

"Looks like I'm in luck!" Sunita muttered to the others. The girls all sat at the same table, and although it was very close to the teacher's desk, Ms Drury was busy over by the door, pinning some project work to the walls. The teacher had asked them to write stories this morning, so Sunita carefully spread her design out under cover of her English book, and opened her pencil case.

The classroom was silent as the girls worked on their writing, and Sunita found it easy to concentrate on her design. She didn't think the line of the top was quite right, and wanted to improve it. But she had to keep stopping every five minutes or so to write a few sentences in her English book. She didn't want Ms Drury becoming suspicious.

"What are you up to, Banerjee?"

The voice in her ear made Sunita almost jump out of her skin. Alex Marshall, the bully who had made Carli's first few weeks at the school a nightmare not long ago, was standing next to her and looking over her shoulder.

"Nothing!" Sunita snapped, pushing the design out of sight under her English book. "Now get lost!"

Alex grinned. "Oh dear," she gloated, "looks like little goody-goody Banerjee's doing something she shouldn't!"

"Shove off, Alex!" Lauren warned her angrily

under her breath, glancing across the room to make sure Ms Drury wasn't watching. But it was too late.

"What are you doing out of your seat, Alex?" All the girls looked over at Ms Drury, who was bustling across the room towards them with a frown.

"I came to get a ruler, Miss," Alex said virtuously, "and I just happened to see Sunita drawing a picture when she should be writing her story."

Ms Drury fixed Sunita with a stare. "Are you getting on with your story or not, Sunita?"

Sunita didn't trust herself to speak, so she just pointed at her English book.

"She was drawing, Miss," Alex insisted gleefully. "I saw her put it under her book!"

Sunita began to tremble all over. If Ms Drury saw her design, it would be confiscated, no question. What could she do then? She wouldn't have a chance of entering the competition. Sunita could hardly breathe as Ms Drury leaned over, and, with a grim look on her face, picked up her English book.

But the piece of paper had gone.

Sunita could hardly believe her eyes, and neither could Alex. They both stared down at the spot where the drawing had been with their mouths wide open.

"Well, that's settled that," said Ms Drury, eyeing Alex Marshall coldly. "Now, go back to your seat."

"I'll get you for that, Banerjee!" Alex muttered in a poisonous voice before she stormed off. The girls stayed quiet until Ms Drury had gone, and then Sunita looked round at them.

"What happened?" she whispered.

Lauren lifted up her own English book, and quickly slid Sunita's drawing back across the table towards her.

"I whipped it out when you were all watching Ms Drury heading straight for us," she confessed, with a smile. "I knew Alex would try to drop you in it."

"Thanks, Lauren," Sunita said gratefully. She took the design, and put it quickly into her bag.

"Aren't you going to finish it?" Carli asked.

Sunita shook her head. "I'll leave it till lunch-time. One narrow escape is enough!"

Sunita had never known a day at school go by quite so fast. She'd managed to work on her design at break and at lunch-time, although Alex and her friends had guessed that something was going on, and kept trying to find out what she was doing. Gemma, Lauren and Carli did their best to shield her from their nasty comments, but it wasn't easy. By the end of the day Sunita still hadn't finished. In desperation, she pretended she had a stomach-ache to get out of PE, the last lesson of the afternoon, and that gave her another forty-five minutes. She put the last touches to her entry as the home bell rang out, and was just sealing up the envelope as Lauren, Gemma and Carli came hurrying back to the classroom to find her.

"Did you finish it?" Gemma asked anxiously.

Sunita nodded, looking tired. "Yeah, about thirty seconds ago. Come on, let's go!"

The four girls grabbed their bags and hurried out into the playground. There was a post-box just outside the gate, and Sunita stuck a stamp on the envelope.

"I need loads of luck!" she said, holding out her little fingers to the others. They all linked up to make a circle.

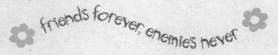

friends forever, enemies never

As they finished their chant, Sunita kissed the envelope for luck and pushed it through the slot.

45

"That's it!" she said with a sigh of relief. "I didn't think I was going to make it. Thanks for all your help. I couldn't have done it without you."

"You wouldn't have got it done at all if Alex had had anything to do with it," Lauren said. "I almost punched her on the nose when she wouldn't leave you alone!"

"Have you told your mum and dad about the competition?" Carli asked, pushing her glasses up her nose with an ink-stained hand.

Sunita shook her head. "I'll tell them if I'm a finalist, but I probably won't be, so there's no need for them to know."

"Maybe you should tell them now," Carli suggested. "They'll go mad if they find out later."

"No," Sunita said firmly. "They'll just give me loads of hassle about it. Anyway, I bet I don't even make it to the finals, so what's the point of telling them?" She shrugged. "What Mum and Dad don't know won't hurt them…"

Chapter 5

"I think we've got biscuit-eating aliens living in this house!"

Gemma, Sunita and Anya, who were pouring themselves glasses of orange juice, looked at Mrs Gordon in amazement.

"Look!" Mrs Gordon up-ended the biscuit tin, and a few crumbs fell out on to the worktop. "There were at least three unopened packets of biscuits in here yesterday, so where've they all gone? It's like something out of *The X-Files*!"

"I haven't eaten them," Gemma said quickly.

Mrs Gordon shook her head in exasperation. "And where's that bottle of Coca-Cola? It was here this morning."

Gemma shrugged. "What're you asking me for? I haven't touched it!"

"Oh, well, I can guess who the real culprit is," Mrs Gordon said, raising her eyebrows as someone opened the front door and came in. "Talk of the devil…"

"Hi, everyone!" Gemma's dad came into the kitchen in his overalls, smelling of engine oil as usual. "Got anything to eat, love? I'm starving!"

The girls began to giggle at the look on Mrs Gordon's face.

"Here!" Mrs Gordon thrust the empty biscuit tin into her husband's hands. "You'd better eat this because it's all that's left!"

"Well, what are you blaming me for?" Garry Gordon asked, looking injured. "I don't want biscuits, anyway. How about a bacon sandwich?"

Mrs Gordon sighed. "I think everyone in this family must have hollow legs!" she remarked, opening the fridge. "Well, you're in luck. Obviously the aliens don't like bacon!"

"What?" Mr Gordon looked bewildered.

"Don't worry about it, Dad!" Gemma laughed as she, Sunita and Anya left the room.

"I wonder if they'll have anything on about the competition this week," Sunita remarked as they sat down in front of the TV. They had been watching *Live on Saturday* since Sunita and Anya had arrived, but nothing had been mentioned so far.

"How long did you say you'd have to wait for the results?" Gemma asked, turning the volume up a little.

Sunita pulled a face. "About four weeks from now."

"Four weeks!" Gemma exclaimed. "That's forever!"

"I know," Sunita sighed, "I've even made a calendar so I can cross the days off one by one!"

"Good idea," Anya said. "I think I'll do that."

"Gran found it and wanted to know what it was, so I told her I was counting down to a big maths test at school!" Sunita grinned. "She was dead impressed!"

Gemma laughed. "Well, Lauren's been going crazy waiting for a letter from the district team. I think she's counting the minutes, never mind the days!" The doorbell rang then, and she jumped up. "That'll be Carli."

When Gemma opened the door, both Carli and Annie were waiting outside, and their mum, Mrs Pike, was walking away down the path.

"See you later!" she called over her shoulder.

"Annie!" Lucy appeared at the top of the stairs, as the girls were taking off their coats. "Come up quick, I want to show you something!"

"What?" Gemma asked suspiciously, but Lucy just

Spotlight on Sunita

stuck her tongue out at her. Annie hurried upstairs, and the two little girls disappeared into Lucy's bedroom, slamming the door shut behind them.

"What on earth are they up to?" Gemma asked Carli.

Carli shrugged. "I don't know. Maybe they've started a secret gang or something."

"Lucy's driving me mad," Gemma went on, as they went into the living-room. "She's acting so smug, as if she knows something I don't."

"Oh, don't let it get you down!" Carli said. "Hello, Sunita. Hi, Anya."

"Hi, Carli – oh, rats!" Sunita sat bolt upright, looking dismayed as the *Live on Saturday* credits began to roll. "It's finished, and they didn't even mention the competition once!"

"We didn't see the beginning, maybe it was on then," Anya suggested.

"Gemma?" Mrs Gordon looked round the door. "I'm going to pop down to the corner shop while your dad's here on his break. Go and ask Lucy and Annie if they want a drink, will you?"

"Oh, Mum," Gemma began, but Mrs Gordon just gave her a warning look, and went out.

Gemma raced upstairs two at a time, and flung open Lucy's bedroom door without knocking. Lucy and Annie were lying on the carpet painting, but

50

as Gemma burst in, they grabbed their pictures and hid them behind their backs.

"What're you two up to?" Gemma demanded suspiciously.

"Nothing!" Lucy retorted.

Gemma stared hard at the two younger girls. Annie turned pink and looked away, but Lucy glared defiantly at her sister. Gemma wondered whether she should try to find out what was going on, because something obviously was, but then she decided against it. It would only mean more trouble from her mum.

"Mum wants to know if you want a drink," she said, and then her eyes widened in angry disbelief. "You've got my paints!"

"We're only borrowing them!" Lucy shouted.

"But I didn't say you could!" Gemma yelled angrily. "Give them back!"

"No, we need them!"

Lucy and Gemma both lunged for the paintbox, while Annie backed away, looking scared. They both got hold of one end of it, and began pulling.

"Let go!" Gemma shouted. "They're mine!"

"But we *need* them!" Lucy wailed.

"Gems?" Sunita called up the stairs, "Lauren's just got back from the match. Shall we go to the park now?"

Gemma let go of the paintbox so suddenly that Lucy tumbled backwards onto her bed.

"I'll deal with you later," Gemma snapped, and hurried downstairs.

"Three-nil! Three-nil! Three-nil!" Lauren sang loudly as Mrs Standish pulled up outside the house. "And who scored all the goals? I did!"

"Oh, get a life, why don't you," grumbled her older brother Ben as he climbed out of the car. "You haven't shut up since we left the sports centre!"

"Don't be such a misery-guts!" Lauren retorted, thinking it was a shame Suzanne Thornton hadn't been there to see her performance today. She'd played even better than last week. "It's not my fault your team lost two-one!"

Ben groaned. "Stop going on about it, will you? If I hadn't missed that penalty…"

"You should have come over to our pitch and asked me to take it for you!" Lauren teased him as they went up the garden path. "Then the goalie wouldn't have stood a chance!"

She pretended to kick an imaginary ball, and took the head clean off a daffodil. Mrs Standish, who was following with Lauren and Ben's baby brother,

Harry, in her arms, tried to look stern, but she couldn't help smiling.

"I don't know how I stand living in a house with all you football-mad people!" she sighed as she unlocked the door and Bart the dog charged up the hallway to greet them, barking loudly. "Never mind, maybe Harry'll be different!"

She put the toddler down, and Harry immediately made a bee-line for the dog's rubber ball, which was lying in the corner. He kicked it down the hall, and it flew through the kitchen doorway.

"Goal!" Harry roared and raced after it, with Bart in hot pursuit. Mrs Standish shook her head, while Ben and Lauren collapsed with laughter.

"Sorry, Mum!" Ben said. "Looks like Harry's already caught football fever!"

"That means I'll be washing muddy football kits for the next fifteen years at least!" Mrs Standish sighed, as the telephone rang. She picked up the receiver, sticking a finger in her ear to cut out the sound of Harry and Bart chasing each other round the kitchen. "Hello?" Then she turned to Lauren. "It's for you, love. It's Suzanne Thornton!"

"Oh!" Lauren dropped her sports bag and leapt forward, her face lighting up. "Hello?"

"Hello, Lauren," Suzanne said. "I was very impressed with your performance at the match last weekend. We're having trials for the district team next Thursday, and I was wondering if you'd like to come along."

"I'd love to!" Lauren gasped, trembling all over with excitement.

"Good." Suzanne gave her a few more details and then rang off, saying, "I look forward to seeing you then."

"I'll be there!" Lauren assured her fervently before she put the phone down. Even an earthquake wouldn't keep her away!

"Yes! I've been asked to try out for the team!" she yelled, punching the air in delight. "The trials are next Thursday!"

"Brilliant!" Ben slapped his sister on the back, and Mrs Standish gave her a hug.

"Fantastic, Lauren, well done!" she exclaimed. "Your dad's going to be thrilled."

"Not as thrilled as I am!" Lauren hugged her mother back. "I'm so happy, I could cartwheel right up the road and back!"

"That *would* make Mrs Crick's eyes pop out!" said Mrs Standish, with a chuckle. Mrs Crick was the nosy woman who lived across the road and spied on everybody from behind her net curtains.

"Mum, can I go next door and tell Gemma?" Lauren asked breathlessly, diving for the door without waiting for an answer. At the same moment that she threw open the front door, the Gordons' front door opened too, and Gemma and the others came out.

"Hey, you lot!" Lauren shouted, charging up the Gordons' path towards them. "You'll never guess what – I've been asked to try out for the district team!"

"Ooh, brill!" Gemma squealed, giving Lauren a hug.

"That's great!" said Sunita and Carli together.

"I'm really pleased for you, Lauren," Anya added.

"Come in, and we'll celebrate before we go to the park," Gemma said, leading the way back into her house.

"First I score a hat-trick, and now I might be playing for the district team!" Lauren flopped down on the sofa, and grinned at the others. "I can hardly stand the excitement!"

"What's all the noise about?" Mr Gordon walked into the living-room, a half-eaten bacon sandwich in his hand.

"I've got a trial for the district team," Lauren told him.

"And we're going to celebrate," Gemma added. "If I can find any food and drink to celebrate *with*!" The girls giggled, and Mr Gordon groaned.

"You're as bad as your mother! I keep telling her I haven't eaten any of this stuff that's gone missing."

"Yeah, right, Dad." Gemma winked at the others. "Shan't be a minute."

Lucy was in the kitchen, looking in one of the cupboards. She was so intent on what she was doing, she didn't hear Gemma walk up behind her.

"BOO!" Gemma said loudly in her ear.

Lucy jumped a mile, dropping the bags of crisps she had in her hands. "Very funny," she snapped.

"Are all those for you and Annie?" Gemma looked down at the six packets of crisps on the floor. "Mum'd go *ballistic* if she knew you were eating all that before lunch."

"Why don't you mind your own business, Gemma!" Lucy turned bright red, grabbed the crisps, and flounced out of the room. Gemma stared after her, wondering why her sister had suddenly looked so guilty.

A sudden thought sprang into her mind. Was it *Lucy* who was responsible for all the food that was going missing? Gemma frowned. No, that was stupid. How could Lucy eat all that lot by herself?

But Gemma decided that there was definitely something weird going on. And she was determined to find out what it was.

Chapter 6

"**G**ood luck," Gemma called, as Lauren climbed into her father's car. "We'll be thinking about you!"

"We'll keep our fingers crossed," Carli said.

"We'll keep *everything* crossed!" Sunita added.

"That sounds a bit painful!" Lauren managed a smile, even though her tummy was doing backflips, and waved at them. "Bye!"

Mr Standish had picked Lauren up after school on Thursday to drive her to the ground on the other side of town where the district team were based. Lauren was feeling more nervous every minute, but she kept telling herself that she was bound to do well. After all, she *was* the star striker of the sports centre league.

"Here we are then." Mark Standish drew up

Spotlight on Sunita

outside the ground. "I wish I could come and watch you, love, but no supporters allowed this time, I'm afraid."

"Oh, I'll be fine, Dad," Lauren said as confidently as she could. "Don't worry."

"Well, good luck then. Oh, and Lauren," Mr Standish went on as his daughter climbed out of the car, "don't be too upset if you don't make it this time. There'll be plenty of good players trying out for the team tonight."

"Yeah, sure, Dad," Lauren murmured, hardly hearing a word he said. "See you later."

Lauren got her first shock when she hurried into the changing-rooms to report to Suzanne. The place seemed to be full of girls, twenty of them at least – surely they weren't *all* trying out for the team?

"It's Lauren Standish, isn't it?" Suzanne, in tracksuit and trainers, walked towards her, carrying a clipboard. "Mark's daughter?"

Lauren nodded. "Are all these girls here for the trials?" she asked anxiously.

Suzanne shook her head. "No, we have our regular team here tonight too, for training." Lauren breathed a silent sigh of relief, until Suzanne spoilt it by adding, "There's only ten girls here for trials."

Ten! Lauren's face fell. She'd reckoned there would

58

only be two or three girls trying out besides her.

"Get changed quickly then," said Suzanne with a smile. "We're almost ready to start."

Lauren looked round for somewhere to put her bag on the crowded benches. She spotted a small space, but when she tried to squeeze her bag on to it, she accidentally knocked someone's football boots off the bench.

"Excuse me," said a haughty voice, "but there isn't any room here!"

Lauren looked round and glared at the speaker, a tall, red-haired girl with very white skin peppered with freckles. "Yes there is," she said pointedly. "You just have to move up a bit."

The girl sniffed, grabbed her boots and disappeared out of the changing-room door. Lauren pulled a face at her back, and then quickly began to change into her kit.

Lauren got her second shock a few minutes later when the trials began. The girls were asked to dribble footballs round cones, show off their heading and tackling skills and take penalty kicks. Lauren had always been the star of her junior team in training, but here she was just one of

59

many talented girls. Rebecca King, the snooty redhead, was especially good, very light on her feet and fast with it. Lauren was dismayed to discover that Rebecca was a striker too, just like herself. She was beginning to realise that her automatic entry into the team was not guaranteed – she was really going to have to fight for a place.

"Right," Suzanne said as she gathered all the girls together in the centre circle. "I'll divide you up, and we'll finish off with a quick game."

Lauren was pleased to find that she was not on Rebecca's team. This was her chance to show what she could do.

The game began. Only a few minutes later, Lauren received the ball from one of her team, and swept down the field towards the opposition's goal. The goalkeeper immediately moved out to block the angle, so that Lauren would find it difficult to shoot. Lauren simply avoided her, dribbling the ball skilfully to one side, and booted it into the net.

"Well done, Lauren!" Suzanne called, making a note on her clipboard.

Lauren glowed with pleasure. But it was short-lived. Five minutes later Rebecca King got the ball, beat two of Lauren's team with a dazzling display of footwork and then gently chipped the ball over the goalie's head. It flew up, and dipped down just below the crossbar.

"Very good, Rebecca!" Suzanne shouted approvingly, and Lauren's heart sank. There was no getting away from it – Rebecca King was a good player, and the district team wouldn't have a place for more than one striker...

"Everything OK?" Mr Standish asked when he picked his daughter up after the trials.

"Yeah," Lauren muttered gloomily. "Fine."

Her father looked sympathetic. "I did warn you that the other players would all be good as well," he said, as the car moved off.

"I didn't realise *how* good..."

When they arrived home, Mrs Standish took one look at her daughter's face and frowned. "Oh, come on, love, it couldn't have been that bad, could it?"

"It was." Lauren sat down at the kitchen table, and put her head in her hands. "I was rubbish."

"I saw you get back!" Gemma rushed into the kitchen behind Mr Standish, stepping over Harry who was sitting on the floor playing with his train set. "So how did it go?"

Her voice faded away as she saw Lauren

Spotlight on Sunita

slumped dispiritedly at the table.

"I did OK," Lauren muttered, "I just didn't do *brilliantly*."

"I thought you said you scored a goal?" Mr Standish pointed out.

"Well, you must have done all right then!" Gemma exclaimed.

Lauren brightened up a little. "Yeah," she said. "I suppose so..."

"When will you know if you've made the team?" Mrs Standish asked.

"Suzanne said I'd get a letter in a few days time." Lauren turned to Gemma. "Come on, let's go upstairs."

"I'm going to go *bananas* waiting for that letter to come!" Lauren said when they were sprawled out on her bed.

"At least you don't have to wait very long," Gemma pointed out. "Anya and Sunita have still got three weeks to wait for the finals of the competition!"

"I'd have no fingernails left if I had to wait till then!" Lauren said. "Sunita seems to be handling it OK, though."

"Well, you know what she's like. She can cope with most things."

"Except maybe her gran!" Lauren said with a smile. "Have you sussed out what's going on with Lucy yet?"

Gemma shook her head. "No. But you know what? Whatever it is, it'll mean trouble for me!"

Lauren grinned. "I never thought I'd see the day when you were frightened of a seven-year-old!" she teased.

Gemma grinned back reluctantly. "I know it sounds daft. But I'm sure there's something going on, and whatever it is, Annie Pike's in on it too!"

"Have you told your mum you think it's Lucy who's been nicking all the food?" Lauren asked.

Gemma nodded. "I told Mum I saw her taking all those crisps, but she said there was no way Lucy could be eating all the stuff that's going missing."

"But you reckon something funny's going on?" Lauren raised her eyebrows.

"Definitely. There's still food disappearing, for a start. I had a sneaky look round Lucy's bedroom yesterday, but I didn't find anything."

"Oh, well, it can't be anything very interesting, whatever it is," Lauren said with a yawn. "After all, she and Annie are only kids."

"Yeah, you're right." Gemma shrugged. "It just bugs me that I don't know what she's up to!"

"Lauren! Will you please come away from the door?" Mrs Standish called down the hallway. "You'll give the postman a heart attack if you hang around there like that!"

"Where is he, anyway?" Lauren asked, peering through the letterbox. "He's late!"

"Come and have some breakfast," Mr Standish said. "We've got to leave for the sports centre in half an hour."

"I couldn't eat a thing!" Lauren looked through the letterbox again. "The letter's got to come this morning, Dad – it's *got* to!"

"You only had the trial two days ago!" Ben remarked, as he came down the stairs with his sports bag.

"I know, but Suzanne said she'd be in touch really quickly." Lauren spun round at the sound of the garden gate opening. "That's him!"

"Let's hope it's arrived," Ben teased her. "You're driving me crazy!"

Bart had heard the postman arriving too, and he charged up the hallway, barking joyously.

"Sorry, Bart," Lauren said, pushing him away, "Me first!"

Four envelopes fell through the letterbox, and

Lauren caught them before they hit the mat. She sorted quickly through them, then waved a long, white envelope above her head.

"This is it!" she yelled.

"Hurry up, I'm dying to know what it says!" her mum said, rushing out of the kitchen with Harry in her arms and Mr Standish close behind her.

Lauren ripped the envelope open, and pulled the letter out with shaking fingers. She scanned the first few lines, and then gave a shout of joy.

"We are pleased to tell you that you have been selected for the district team squad – YES! Mum, Dad, I did it!"

"That's fantastic, love!" said Mrs Standish, giving her a hug.

Lauren skimmed down the rest of the letter. "We would like you to report to the manager for training next week on Tuesday and Thursday at the team's ground to prepare for the match against Burton Rovers on Saturday. You'll be..." Lauren stopped reading, and her face fell.

"What's the matter?" her father asked.

"You'll be one of the *substitutes*," Lauren read out, her voice shaking with disappointment. "Oh, Dad, I'm not in the team after all – I'm only a substitute!"

Chapter 7

Lauren banged on the Gordons' front door. She had rushed straight round to talk to Gemma about the letter which had ruined her hopes and dreams. So she was only good enough to be the sub, and not in the team at all? Well, she wasn't going to stand for it!

Carli opened the door.

"Oh," Lauren said, disappointed. "What're you doing here? Where's Gemma?"

"I came over early to clean out the rabbits," Carli replied, wondering what had upset Lauren so much. "Gemma's just gone to the corner shop and Mrs Gordon's upstairs. Do you want to come in?"

"No, I can't wait," Lauren said miserably. "I've got a match this morning."

"Is anything the matter?" Carli asked cautiously.

She knew how quick-tempered Lauren could be, and she didn't want to wind her up even more.

"I had a letter from the district team," Lauren burst out. She would rather have talked to Gemma, but she couldn't keep it bottled up any longer. "They've asked me to be a substitute! I can't believe it!"

"And are you going to?"

Lauren tossed her head haughtily. "No, of course not!" she exclaimed. "I mean, I get to play every week with the sports centre team. I *never* have to sit on the bench!"

"But if you say no, maybe the district team won't ask you to go for trials again," Carli said carefully.

"Well, that's their problem!" Lauren snapped.

"I just thought..." Carli swallowed hard, and forced herself to go on. Lauren looked so fierce, she couldn't help feeling a little scared of her. "I just thought that if you were the substitute, you'd probably get a chance to go on and show them what you can do. Then you might get a place in the real team."

Lauren opened her mouth to argue, and then closed it again as Carli's words sank in. She was right. Turning down the offer of playing substitute could mean she'd never get another chance with the district team. At least there was a chance of playing part of a match as the sub, and then she could do her best to impress the manager.

Lauren nodded. "You could be right," she said reluctantly. "I'll think about it, anyway. Thanks, Carli…"

"See you tomorrow then, Lauren!" Gemma said cheerfully as she and Sunita climbed out of the Standishes' car. "And good luck with your training session tonight!"

Lauren scowled. "I'm only the sub, anyway. Suzanne probably won't care if I turn up or not."

"Of course she will!" Sunita said. "What if someone goes sick and can't play?"

"Oh, big deal!" Lauren muttered, slumping down in her seat. At first she had decided that Carli was right, and she ought not to lose this opportunity, but over the last few days she had begun to regret her decision. Still, it was too late now. She had already told her previous team that she was leaving.

"Bye, girls," Mrs Standish said, but Lauren didn't say anything.

"Ouch!" Gemma said ruefully as she and Sunita went up to the Banerjees' front door. They had decided to do their homework together at Sunita's place that evening. "I don't think Lauren's too happy about only being the sub!"

"Carli's right, though." Sunita fished in her pocket for her key. "At least if Lauren's in the squad, she's got a chance of making the team."

"Mmm. Lauren's not used to being second-best though – especially at football..."

"That was a bit mean, Lauren," Mrs Standish was saying as she turned into their street. "Gemma and Sunita were only trying to help."

"I know," Lauren said in a low voice. She was already feeling ashamed of herself, but no one seemed to understand how she felt...

Lauren trailed into the house, changed out of her school uniform and packed her sports bag with none of the anticipation she usually felt when she had a training session to go to. *Why* hadn't she turned down the district team, she asked herself miserably for the hundredth time. She might never get a full game, and then she'd be stuck sitting on the subs' bench for ever. It was all Carli's fault...

Lauren was in a bad mood by the time her mum dropped her off at the ground, and when she

walked into the changing-rooms, it didn't improve. There were only a couple of girls in there, and the first person she saw was Rebecca King, sitting on the bench pulling on her socks. The red-haired girl stared at her.

"I didn't know *you* were in the team," she said snootily.

"I'm not," Lauren muttered, her cheeks burning with embarrassment. "I'm the sub."

A smirk spread over Rebecca King's freckled face. "Oh dear, what a shame," she said jauntily, and turned away.

Lauren stomped over to a spare bench, and flung her bag down on it. She wanted to walk out of there right away and go back home, but she knew that would seem totally unprofessional. Even so… she couldn't *bear* the thought of Rebecca having a laugh at her expense, and she wasn't going to spend Saturday after Saturday sitting on the bench when she could be enjoying herself with her old team. No way.

'I've had enough of this,' Lauren thought miserably as she took her kit out. 'I'm going to ring my old team and ask for my place back.'

"Hello, Lauren!" Suzanne hurried into the dressing-room, looking pleased to see her. "Great to have you here." Briskly, she ticked Lauren's name off the list on her clipboard. "Now will you be able to make the training session on Thursday, too?"

"I'm not sure," Lauren muttered, knowing that somehow she had to find the courage to tell the manager straight out that she wasn't interested in playing for the team any more.

Suzanne looked dismayed. "Have you got something else on? Because you've got to come to training regularly if you want to be in the team. I was thinking of playing you in the match against Hampton United a week on Saturday."

Lauren stared at her. "You – you mean I'll get a chance to play in the team?" she stammered. "I won't have to be a sub all the time?"

Suzanne shook her head with a puzzled smile. "Of course not! It's team policy to change the subs around regularly to give everyone a chance."

A big grin spread across Lauren's face. "I'll see you on Thursday, then!" she said happily, relief flooding through her. Thank goodness she hadn't opened her big mouth and said she didn't want to be in the team! And it was a good job she hadn't turned down the sub's place when she'd received the letter, too – that was all down to Carli's good advice.

'Thank you, Carli!' she thought joyfully, 'Thank you, thank you, thank you!'

"Oh, those fractions were *gruesome*, Gems," Sunita groaned, closing her maths book. She got up from the desk, and flopped down onto her bed. "Good thing you were here to help me – I hadn't got a clue!"

Gemma grinned. "Oh, they weren't that bad."

"I'll never understand why you like maths so much," Sunita said, shaking her head. "I mean, you *look* pretty normal..."

"Hey, watch it!" Gemma poked her with a ruler. "There's nothing strange about liking maths!"

"Yeah, right!" Sunita snorted. "I wonder how Lauren's getting on?"

"Who knows?" Gemma shrugged. "In the mood she's in, she's probably half-killed someone!"

Sunita giggled. "D'you want to stay for tea, Gems?"

"I'd love to, but I've got to get home," Gemma sighed. "Mum's working tonight, and I promised to help Dad look after Lucy. I'm still trying to find out what the little monster's up to."

"Is there still loads of food going missing?"

"No, but that's because I reckon Lucy knows I'm on to her. I still haven't worked out what she's playing at, though."

"Hey, Gems, you don't think Lucy's planning to

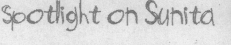

run away, do you?" Sunita said suddenly. "That might be why she's saving up all that food."

Gemma suddenly looked alarmed. "I don't know. I hadn't thought of that."

Sunita burst out laughing. "Well, she won't get very far with all those bags of crisps and bottles of Coke to carry!" Then she stopped as she saw Gemma's stricken face. "Oh, come on, Gems, I was joking! You don't *really* think that?"

"Well, it all fits, doesn't it?" Gemma said in a shaky voice. "I don't know why I didn't think of it before…"

Sunita looked doubtful. "Lucy wouldn't do that," she said, but then paused. "Would she?"

"I don't know." Gemma suddenly felt very cold all over. "But I've got to find out!"

"Look, Gems," Sunita began, but she was talking to thin air. Gemma had grabbed her bag and rushed out of the room.

Maybe she *was* being silly, Gemma told herself as she raced home. But what if it was true? What if her sister really was planning to run away because of all the fights she and Gemma had had? Gemma would never forgive herself…

Spotlight on Sunita

She let herself in and hurried upstairs, two at a time, to Lucy's bedroom. Lucy had stuck a sign reading *Privet* on to the door, but even Lucy's terrible spelling couldn't make Gemma smile. She took a deep breath, flung open the door and rushed into the room.

Her sister was sitting on the floor with a huge banner and paint pots and brushes spread out all around her. Gemma had a confused glimpse of brightly-coloured letters reading 'Happy Birthday, Carli!', just before she tripped over a pot of dirty water holding the brushes and went sprawling onto the bed. The water cascaded all over the banner, smudging the word 'Birthday' into a pink blur.

"Look what you've done!" Lucy shouted, and burst into tears.

"S-sorry," Gemma stammered, still not sure what on earth was going on.

"You should have knocked!" Lucy sobbed. "I said it was private!"

"Maybe we can fix it." Quickly Gemma got down on her knees, and began mopping up the mess with some material nearby.

"That's my school blouse!" Lucy roared, outraged.

"Sorry." Gemma hurried to the bathroom and grabbed a roll of toilet paper. She tried to clear the water up, but it was obvious that the banner was ruined. Lucy watched her, still crying.

"I'm really sorry," Gemma said again. "But what are you doing?"

Lucy wiped her eyes and stared at her defiantly. "Me and Annie decided to have a surprise party for Carli's birthday."

"What?" Gemma was amazed. She hadn't even known Carli's birthday was coming up.

Lucy nodded. "We wanted to show you we weren't just little kids," she said in a small voice. "I've been collecting loads of food and drink. Look!" She reached under her bed and pulled out a box which was packed with all sorts of things. "Annie's got some too," she added proudly.

Gemma wanted to laugh, but she was also quite touched. It was a lovely idea on Lucy and Annie's part, even if they had gone about it in a funny way.

"Mum thinks Dad's eating it all!" she said. "When is Carli's birthday, anyway?"

"In two or three weeks," Lucy sniffled, wiping her wet face.

"She didn't say," Gemma remarked thoughtfully.

"Annie said she didn't want anyone to know. Look, we've made cards and decorations too," Lucy went on. "And we've bought some balloons with our pocket-money."

"I think you've done a brilliant job," Gemma said, and Lucy smiled through her tears. "So will you let us all help you now? With the party, I mean. I can help you to make another banner for a start."

Lucy looked surprised and pleased. "All right," she agreed.

"And we could tell Mum," Gemma suggested. "She'll probably make a birthday cake. And I bet the other girls will want to help too."

Lucy nodded happily. "I'll get some more paper," she said.

As Gemma helped Lucy to sellotape clean sheets of paper together to make another banner, she realised that it was the first time in ages they'd worked together on something without arguing. She should have listened to Carli earlier, she thought. Maybe her sister wasn't *quite* so bad after all...

It was amazing how Carli always seemed to give such good advice, Gemma thought as she painted *Happy Birthday* in big, pink letters. She might be quiet, but she certainly didn't miss much. She deserved to have a really excellent party, and Gemma knew that the other girls would feel exactly the same way when she told them.

Chapter 8

"**S**o what's this big secret you need to discuss with us, Gemma?" Anya swam neatly to the side of the sports centre pool, then jumped out of the way as Lauren leapt from the diving-board, splashing everyone around her. "Do you mind," she snapped. "I don't want to get my hair wet!"

"Oh, leave it out!" Lauren gasped, coming up for air. "How can you go swimming and *not* get your hair wet?"

"Easy!" Anya retorted. "I just keep away from idiots like you!"

"Shut up, you two!" Gemma said, treading water next to them. "This is important."

"Well, if it's *that* important, why didn't you phone us?" Anya asked grumpily.

"And you could have told me and Sunita at

Spotlight on Sunita

school today," Lauren pointed out.

"I wanted us all to be together to talk about it," Gemma said patiently.

"Well, Carli's not here," Anya persisted.

"This is *about* Carli."

The girls had already arranged to go swimming, and Gemma had decided that, as Carli couldn't come because she was going to tea with her father, it would be the perfect time to discuss the party plans. She turned to see where Sunita had got to. She was floating on her back, staring up at the ceiling as if she was on another planet. "Sunita!"

Sunita didn't hear her.

"SUNITA!"

"Oh, sorry." Sunita swam over to them. "I was just thinking about –"

"The competition!" Lauren and Gemma said together, smiling.

Sunita sighed. "I know I'm being boring, but there's only two weeks to go until they announce the finalists! I just can't concentrate on anything else!"

"Me neither," Anya announced. "Wouldn't it be awesome if we *both* made the finals?"

Gemma saw Lauren open her mouth to say something, and quickly nudged her under the water.

"Look, I wanted us to get together to talk about Carli's birthday party."

"What?" Anya asked, and Gemma explained.

"So that's what those little toads were up to!" Lauren said with a grin, rolling over onto her back. "They were nicking food to have a party for Carli!"

Sunita laughed. "I think that's sweet!"

"I wonder why Carli didn't tell us her birthday's coming up soon?" Anya asked, puzzled.

"Well, I don't know for sure," Gemma said slowly, "but I'd guess Carli's a bit embarrassed because her mum can't afford to take us all out. You know how we all went ice-skating and to that pizza restaurant for your birthday a couple of months ago..."

"Poor Carli!" Sunita looked upset. "So we're going to have a party for her?"

Gemma nodded. "Yeah, but it was Lucy and Annie's idea, so I think we ought to let them organise it and tell us what to do! Mum said we can have it at our house – she was dead relieved when she found out the real reason why all that food had been disappearing!"

"I want to get Carli a really *brilliant* present," said Lauren. "If it wasn't for her, I'd have lost my chance to play for the district team."

"I'm hoping Snowball's going to have babies,"

Gemma said with a grin. "That'd be a fantastic present, but I don't think they'll be born in time for the party."

"Oh!" Sunita gasped, her face suddenly lighting up, "I've got a fab idea – I could design a dress for her!"

"Good one, Sunita!" Gemma said, delighted. "We could all club together and pay for the material. It wouldn't cost too much."

Anya pouted. "Why can't *I* design the dress?"

Gemma thought fast. "Because Lucy and Annie will need some help to design and organise the decorations. You know how good you are at that sort of thing."

"Oh, all right," Anya agreed happily.

"A pale pink might be a good colour," Sunita went on, quickly becoming absorbed in her new project. "Or blue. Or maybe green, to go with her lovely green eyes. I'll talk to Carli's mum. She'll be able to help."

Gemma chuckled. "Looks like dreaming up a new creation was all you needed to take your mind off the competition!"

"What competition?" Sunita asked with a smile.

"Well, I can't wait to see what you come up with for Carli!" Lauren said, diving underwater to grab Anya's legs and tip her over.

"You ratbag, Lauren!" Anya spluttered crossly as she surfaced, her hair soaking wet. "I'll get you for that!"

"Sunita, where are you going?" Gemma called as Sunita hauled herself out of the pool.

"I'm going to start right away!" Sunita called back. "This dress has got to be something special!"

"How're you feeling, Sunita?" Lauren asked as she, Sunita and Gemma went into the Gordons' living-room. "You must be nervous."

"I'm *terrified*!" Sunita tried to smile, but her face felt as if it was frozen.

This morning the competition finalists were going to be announced on *Live on Saturday*. Sunita had almost forgotten about it over the last two weeks because of all the preparations for the party but now, all of a sudden, the big day had arrived.

"Have a look at this before Carli gets here," Sunita said, pulling a piece of paper from her pocket and showing it to the others. "I'm sorry it's taken me so long, but I wanted to get it just right."

Gemma and Lauren looked eagerly at the dress Sunita had drawn. It was short and summery with thin shoulder-straps and a flared skirt, and was

81

made of a silky blue material.

"It's perfect!" Gemma said. "It'll really suit her."

"She'll love it!" Lauren added.

"Thanks." Sunita looked pleased. "Mrs Pike's going to help me make it up –" The doorbell rang then, and Sunita quickly stuffed the paper into her pocket. A moment later Anya and Carli came in.

"Quick, put the telly on!" Anya squealed with a glance at the clock. "It's time!"

Lauren switched the TV on, just as the credits of *Live on Saturday* began.

"Turn it up!" Sunita yelled. "I can hardly hear it!"

"I can't find the remote!" Gemma wailed.

"Anya's sitting on it!" Lauren shouted, giving Anya a shove.

"Hey, watch it!" Anya retorted loudly, shoving her back.

Gemma retrieved the remote control and turned the volume up so loud that Eva Jones's voice blasted out into the room, and the girls had to cover their ears.

"– AND A LITTLE LATER IN THE SHOW WE'LL HAVE THE RESULTS OF OUR YOUNG FASHION DESIGNER OF THE YEAR COMPETITION!"

"Ow!" Gemma winced, and turned the sound down again.

"Later in the show?" Sunita said in disgust. "That means we'll have to sit through loads of boring cartoons first!"

"Oh, rats!" Lauren groaned, "I've got to go soon or I'll be late for my match! I hope I don't miss the results..."

They sat through the first cartoon, all of them fidgeting with impatience, and Lauren kept glancing at the clock.

"I'm going to have to shoot off now," she said gloomily, just as Eva Jones announced: "And now for the results of our Young Fashion Designer of the Year Competition!"

"At last!" Sunita gasped. She was shaking so much she was sure that if she stood up, she'd fall over.

"Get a move on!" Anya shouted, as Eva went on and on about how many entries they'd had, and how wonderful they all were.

"Yes, hurry up!" added Lauren, who was standing in the doorway clutching her sports bag. "Some of us have got a district team match to go to!"

"And our three finalists are firstly, Julia Simpson, aged 15, from Manchester..."

"Oh, that's gorgeous," Sunita said as Eva Jones held up the first finalist's design to the camera. It was a lime-green trouser-suit with black trimmings.

"Not as good as yours though," Lauren said quickly.

Anya sniffed. "Nor mine," she said, pointedly.

"And our second finalist is…"

The five girls in the room held their breath.

"…Karl Holt, aged 14, from Norwich!"

"A *boy*?" said Anya, in amazement.

"Well, why not?" said Gemma. "Loads of fashion designers are men!"

Karl's design was a black evening dress with a low-cut neck and a full skirt.

"That's lovely too," Sunita said bravely, as Eva picked up another piece of paper.

"And our third – and last – finalist is quite a lot younger: she's only ten years old. Her name is Sunita Banerjee, from Duston, and this is her very unusual design…"

There was a stunned silence in the Gordons' living-room for about two seconds, and then there was uproar as everyone screamed at once.

"YES!" Sunita squealed. "I did it! I did it! I did it!"

Beaming with delight, Lauren dropped her bag and flung both arms round her. "I knew you would! I told you so, didn't I?" she shouted.

"Well done, Sunita!" Carli said, with a glance at

Anya, who was looking very upset.

"Yes, it's fantastic!" Gemma agreed. "Sorry you didn't make it to the finals, Anya, but you heard what Eva said – there were hundreds of entries."

"Don't worry about it," Anya muttered, but she still looked hurt.

"Just a minute," Sunita gabbled breathlessly, still trying to take in the fact that she was a finalist, "I missed what Eva said next."

They all turned back to the TV, but the competition announcement was over, and another cartoon had started.

"Oh, I wish we'd videoed it, now!" groaned Gemma.

"You're going to be on TV!" Anya said, her voice quivering as she came dangerously close to tears. "You're so lucky, Sunita!"

"Never mind, Anya," Carli said sympathetically, putting her hand on Anya's arm, "Maybe we'll be able to go with her."

Anya cheered up a little. "Yeah, that's true!"

Sunita suddenly slumped in her chair. "If I go," she muttered.

"What do you mean?" Anya looked shocked. "You're going to be on TV – of course you've got to go!"

"I've got to ask my mum and dad first," Sunita

Spotlight on Sunita

said miserably.

"Oh, well, they'll be pleased, won't they?" said Lauren. "I mean, you're in the final, you've been chosen out of hundreds and hundreds of entries!"

Sunita shook her head. "I don't know. I wish I'd taken Carli's advice now, and told them before."

"You'd better not put it off too long then," Gemma advised her. "The programme'll probably be in touch soon."

Sunita nodded unhappily. "I'll do it right now." She stood up, and reached for her jacket. "Wish me luck."

It was only a short walk from Gemma's house to Sunita's, but she made it last as long as she possibly could. Sunita was dreading telling her mum and dad – and especially her gran – that she had entered the competition behind their backs. Still, maybe they'd be so pleased that she was a finalist, they'd forgive her...

Ganesh, Sunita's brother, popped his head out of the kitchen as she let herself in.

"What have you been up to?" he said under his breath, nodding at the living-room door. "They're all going bananas in there!"

Sunita's heart started pounding with fear. Her father looked out into the hall. "Come in here, please, Sunita," he said sternly.

Sunita followed him into the living-room. Her mother and her gran were sitting on the sofa, looking very serious. The TV was on, showing Eva Jones interviewing a famous soap star.

With a feeling of dread, Sunita guessed straight away what had happened. Her parents and her gran had seen the programme.

They knew.

Chapter 9

"We're not happy about this, not happy at all." Mrs Banerjee Senior threw her hands into the air, and stared sternly at Sunita. She had got the shock of her life when she put the TV on that morning, intending to watch the Asian programmes on BBC 2. The channel with *Live on Saturday* had come on just at the moment that Eva Jones was announcing Sunita's name, and Sunita's gran had nearly had hysterics. "You didn't ask for permission to enter this competition."

"I haven't done anything wrong," Sunita muttered. She knew she ought to keep quiet, but she couldn't resist trying to defend herself. "I just did a drawing and sent it in..."

"You did that drawing when you should have been concentrating on your homework," her father snapped, shaking his head. "We've told you a hundred times, you should be spending time on your maths, not on silly pictures."

Sunita looked down at the floor. She wanted to shout, "I hate maths, and my drawings aren't silly!" – but she knew that if she got into an argument now, she could say goodbye to any chance she might have of making it to the final selection on TV, however slight.

"Why didn't you tell us you were entering the competition, Sunita?" her mum asked gently. "We don't like the idea of you doing this behind our backs."

"Because I thought you'd say no," Sunita mumbled, her voice wobbling dangerously. "And I really wanted to have a go. It was important to me."

"I can see that," her father commented, dryly. "You seem to have done pretty well, too."

Sunita looked up hopefully at her dad. He still looked stern, but there had definitely been a note of reluctant pride in his voice. Perhaps there was hope after all...

"Of course that doesn't make it any better," Sunita's gran chimed in, and Sunita's heart sank again.

Just then the door opened, and Ganesh stuck his

head in. "Gran, the curry's burning," he called.

Mrs Banerjee Senior tutted, and stood up, pulling her sari around her. "We're very disappointed in you, Sunita," she announced, and marched majestically off towards the kitchen.

As soon as her gran was out of the room, Sunita seized her chance. "I'm sorry, Dad," she said breathlessly, "I just wanted to have a go, that's all. And I'm not behind with my homework, honestly."

Mr Banerjee sighed. "But your mother's right, Sunita, we don't like the way you went about it."

"I'll never do it again," Sunita said desperately, "I promise! Please, let me go to the studios for the finals…"

Mr Banerjee glanced at his wife, and she shrugged slightly.

"We'll have to think about it," he said at last.

Sunita wanted to argue, but she knew it wouldn't help. "Thanks, Dad," was all she said.

"No promises," her father said sternly. "We're not very pleased with your behaviour, and we're not going to let you go if it interferes with your schoolwork. Now go to your room."

Sunita went upstairs, closed the door and burst into tears. She was going to have to wait and see if she would be allowed to go to the TV studios. What if, in the end, her parents said no? How could she bear it? Why did she *always* have to struggle between two different ways of life, always being forced to follow a path that she didn't want?

The door opened, and her mother came in. "Oh, Sunny, don't cry. Come here."

Sunita flung herself into her mum's arms, feeling as if she was five years old again.

"This is really important to you, isn't it?" Mrs Banerjee asked, as Sunita wiped her eyes with her hand.

Sunita nodded. "I just want to know if I'm any good at designing," she said in a small voice.

"I think you've proved that by being chosen as a finalist." Mrs Banerjee smoothed her daughter's hair back from her face. "But you know what your father's worried about, don't you?"

"He doesn't want me to be a designer," Sunita said gloomily. "But I don't want to be an accountant! I hate maths, Mum!"

Indranee Banerjee sighed. They'd had so many arguments on this subject in the past... She squeezed her daughter's hand. "May I see your design, Sunny?"

Sunita sat up, rubbing at her wet face. "I thought you would have seen it on the programme," she muttered.

Mrs Banerjee shook her head. "No, I was in the

kitchen when it came on," she said, her lips twitching slightly as if she was trying to stop herself from smiling, "I only knew something was going on when your gran started screaming."

"I only kept some rough copies." Sunita picked up her sketchpad, and flipped it open, then handed it to her mother.

Mrs Banerjee's eyes widened. "Sunny, it's a bit like a *shalwar kameez*! It's beautiful!"

"Do you really think so?" Sunita asked eagerly, thrilled that her mother liked the design.

"Yes, I do." Mrs Banerjee stared down at the drawing. "And I'm glad you chose to base your design on an Indian outfit. You know how we worry that your tastes are becoming too western."

"I like both kinds of clothes," Sunita said honestly.

"What's the first prize?" Mrs Banerjee asked as she stood up.

"A day at a fashion designer's studio," Sunita said, "and a new computer."

Mrs Banerjee looked thoughtful. "That might help your father to make up his mind," she said. "He's been thinking of buying a computer for you and the boys for a while, now." She smiled at her daughter. "To help you with your maths, of course."

Sunita felt slightly more cheerful when her mother had gone. Maybe, just maybe, there was a chance that she might make it to the finals after all.

"And we're all very proud of Sunita, and we wish her well in the competition finals!"

The whole school began to clap and cheer, and Sunita forced herself to smile as the headmistress, Mrs Mackintosh, looked at her. She hadn't been prepared for all the fuss that had greeted her when she'd got to school on Monday morning. Everyone knew about the competition, and now here was Mrs Mackintosh announcing it at the end of assembly. Sunita felt sick as she thought about what they would all say if she wasn't allowed to go. She'd never live it down.

Gemma and Lauren, who were standing either side of her, looked at her sympathetically. They knew exactly what Sunita was thinking. Carli, too, was looking anxious.

"What am I going to do?" Sunita asked nervously as the girls filed out of the hall. "Everyone's going to laugh at me if I don't go to the competition finals!"

Spotlight on Sunita

"No, they won't," Gemma began, but just then Alex Marshall and her horrible friends, Marga De Santos and Charlotte Derring, caught up with them.

"Get *you*!" Alex sneered, thrusting her spotty face up close to Sunita's. "I don't know why everyone's getting so excited – you won't win!"

"Get on your broomstick and take a ride, Alex," Gemma snapped.

Alex glared at her. "I'm not talking to you, Gordon!"

"Yeah, mind your own business!" Charlotte snapped. "Alex is right – Sunita the swot won't win!"

Sunita felt like crying, but she choked back the tears. She wouldn't give Alex and her two grinning sidekicks the satisfaction.

Alex, however, had already noticed that something was wrong. "What's up?" she jeered. "Won't your mummy and daddy let you go then?" She was thrilled when her lucky guess hit its target, and Sunita's eyes filled with tears.

"She can't go!" Alex turned to Charlotte and Marga, grinning with malicious delight. "She's not allowed!"

"Shut up, Alex!" shouted Lauren, standing in front of Sunita.

Alex, Charlotte and Marga collapsed into spiteful laughter.

"Come on!" said Marga triumphantly. "Let's go and tell everyone!"

As Alex and her cronies ran off, laughing, Sunita started sobbing. "What am I going to do?" she moaned. "Maybe the programme will choose another finalist if I can't go!"

"I'm sure they won't," Gemma said, trying to console her. "Look, you'll just have to wait and see what your parents say."

Carli took a crumpled tissue from her pocket, and silently offered it to Sunita. Things had been difficult for Carli, lately, with her parents splitting up. Even so, she was beginning to realise just how complicated Sunita's life must be, trying to juggle two different cultures and keep her parents and her gran happy.

Sunita dried her eyes, and tried to smile at the other girls. "Gem's right," she said shakily. "I'll just have to wait and see…"

The rest of the school day was difficult for Sunita and her friends. Alex and her gang were having great fun spreading rumours that Sunita would not be appearing on *Live on Saturday* at all. Sunita was terrified that they might be right, and she developed a terrible headache. She was glad to get home at the end of the day.

"Well, as I said before, we aren't sure yet if we'll be coming." Sunita's mum was on the phone in the hallway when she went in. "But if we did, what time would we need to be at the TV studios?"

Sunita's ears pricked up. That must be someone from *Live on Saturday*! She dropped her bag, and stood waiting to hear what else her mum said, but that was almost the end of the conversation.

"Yes, of course, we'll let you know as soon as possible. I'll ring you back," said Mrs Banerjee, and put down the phone.

"Was that the programme, wanting to know if we're coming?" Sunita asked breathlessly.

Her mum nodded. "It was the researcher, Rachel Nicholls," she said.

"Will they choose another finalist if I can't go?" Sunita asked in a small voice.

"No, don't worry." Mrs Banerjee smiled at her. "You'll still be able to win the competition, whether you're there or not."

But it wouldn't be the *same*, Sunita thought dismally. She wouldn't get to be on TV, nor would she be able to see Eva wearing her outfit for real.

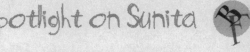

"I think I'd better talk to your father again," Mrs Banerjee decided. "We have to make our minds up one way or another soon."

Sunita looked hopefully at her, but she was giving nothing away.

"Come on," said her mum, putting her arm round her daughter's shoulders. "Gran's in the living-room with Mrs Chopra, and I've just made them some tea. You can take in the tray for me."

Sunita went obediently to the kitchen with her mum, and carried the tea and biscuits into the living-room. As soon as she walked through the door, the two old women started tutting sadly and shaking their heads.

"Girls these days have no shame!" Sunita's gran said bitterly. "They don't know how to behave properly."

"In our day it was different," Mrs Chopra added.

"Hello, Auntie," Sunita said politely. Mrs Chopra wasn't really a relative, she was an old friend of her gran's, but Sunita had always called her auntie. She was hoping to make a quick getaway, but her gran patted the sofa beside her, and Sunita was forced to sit down.

"In our day we didn't show our bodies like they do nowadays," Mrs Chopra went on gloomily. Sunita glanced at her 'auntie', and thought that

97

was just as well – Mrs Chopra had to weigh at least sixteen stone. "We kept ourselves covered up. We didn't care about what was *fashionable*," she added, looking accusingly at Sunita.

The two women lapsed into Hindi then, which Sunita didn't understand very well – especially when it was spoken quickly. She stopped listening, and began to wonder for the millionth time what her mum and dad would decide.

"Sunita's design wasn't so bad." Her gran had reverted back to English now, and was speaking in such a sharp tone of voice, that Sunita looked up, startled. "It wasn't revealing at all."

Mrs Chopra clicked her tongue and shook her head. "Well, it is a good thing she's not going to the finals," she announced self-righteously. "She wouldn't have won anyway!"

"What do you mean?" Mrs Banerjee Senior exclaimed crossly, and the two women were off into Hindi again. Sunita watched them wide-eyed, wishing she could understand what they were saying.

"Sunita will certainly win the competition!" Mrs Banerjee declared finally, in English. "And I'll be going to the TV studios with her!"

Sunita almost bounced out of her seat with surprise. It looked like gran's family pride had finally got the better of her – she couldn't bear to admit to Mrs Chopra that her granddaughter might not be good enough to win the competition! And with Gran on her side, her parents were bound to give in. A great rush of excitement swept over Sunita. She would be on TV, she'd see her design made up... maybe this would be the very first step on the road to her career as a fashion designer!

'Watch out, world, here I come!' Sunita thought, a grin spreading all over her face, 'Sunita Banerjee's on her way right to the top!'

The next day crawled by, but eventually it was time for Carli's birthday party.

"I can't *wait* to be on TV!" Anya said happily, as she fussed around the table rearranging the serviettes. "It's going to be the best day of my whole life!"

"How many times have you said that today?" Lauren remarked, putting on a green party hat. "One million or two?"

Anya pulled a face. "You're just jealous because you can't come with us."

"All right," Lauren sighed, "I admit it, I am. But

I can't let the district team down when I've only just started playing for them."

"It's OK, Lauren, I understand," said Sunita, who was trying to stop Harry from bursting a stray balloon. "But I wish you could be there."

Sunita could still hardly believe it – on Saturday, she, Gemma, Anya and Carli would be going to the TV studios! Mrs Banerjee had managed to get permission for Gemma and the others to be part of *Live on Saturday*'s small studio audience, and Anya had almost fainted with excitement when she'd found out.

"Carli's going to be here in a minute," said Gemma, taking the balloon from Harry and tying it to the door handle. "D'you think she's guessed what's going on?"

Sunita shook her head. "No way!"

Lucy, who had been sitting by the living-room window, keeping a look-out, leapt to her feet. "They're coming!"

"Quiet, everybody!" Gemma said urgently, as Mrs Gordon went to let in Carli, Annie and Mrs Pike.

They all waited in silence. Then, as Carli walked into the living-room, everyone jumped up and shouted, "SURPRISE!"

Carli gasped, completely amazed. The room

was lavishly decorated with balloons, streamers and decorations. A large banner reading 'Happy Birthday, Carli!' hung across the mantelpiece, and there was a long table laden with all kinds of cakes, biscuits and sandwiches in the corner. The room was full of people wearing party hats – Gemma, Anya, Lauren and Sunita, as well as Lucy, Mrs Gordon, Mrs Standish and baby Harry, and Sunita's mum. As Carli stood in the doorway staring around her, Gemma rushed forward and put a silver hat on her head.

"Welcome to your party, Carli!" she cried, giving her a hug. "It was all Lucy and Annie's idea!"

Lucy and Annie grinned with delight.

"It's lovely," Carli said in a trembling voice. She was totally shocked. "Thank you very much!"

"This is for you," said Anya, thrusting a large pink envelope into Carli's hand. Carli tore it open with shaking hands, and pulled out the card inside. There was a fluffy white rabbit on the front, and the words 'To a Very Special Friend.' Carli thought that she might be about to burst into tears of happiness, so she quickly looked at the message inside, blinking hard:

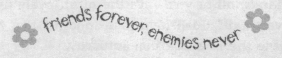
friends forever, enemies never

101

Spotlight on Sunita

All the girls had added a different message underneath. Gemma's read, 'Have a lovely birthday, and congratulations! Snowball's going to be a mum!'

Carli looked amazed. "Snowball's expecting babies – *kittens*, I mean?"

Gemma nodded. "Yep! Sometime in the next week or two."

"I *thought* she was getting fat!" Carli laughed. "You told me she was eating too much!"

"Well, I wanted to keep it a secret until today!" Gemma confessed. "I thought it would be a brilliant present!"

"We've got another present for you too," Sunita said with a smile, handing her a large, flat box.

Inside was something wrapped in gold foil and white tissue paper. Carefully Carli pulled the layers aside.

"Oh!" she gasped. "What a beautiful dress!"

"I designed it!" Sunita said proudly, as Carli lifted the dress out of its wrappings. "And your mum helped me make it up."

"Oh, I didn't do much," Mrs Pike said modestly, "Sunita did most of it!"

"Thanks, all of you – it's the most lovely dress I've ever had!" Carli held it up against her. "I'll wear it to the TV studios on Saturday."

"Just you make sure you look after it," Sunita said teasingly, putting an arm round her friend, as Lucy and Annie started handing round plates of sandwiches. "That's a Sunita Banerjee original, and one day, when I'm a famous fashion designer, it's going to be worth thousands and thousands of pounds!"

Chapter 10

"Oh, this is so exciting!" Anya breathed, clutching Sunita's arm so tightly that her friend winced. "We're really going to be on TV – today! I still can't believe it – pinch me, somebody!"

There was so much to see at the TV studios that the girls couldn't take everything in, and even Sunita's gran seemed overwhelmed. They had arrived in Birmingham early on Saturday morning, and had been met by Rachel, the programme researcher. First she'd taken them down to the canteen for some tea, and then she'd led them along a maze of corridors to the Green Room, where all the *Live on Saturday* guests waited until they were needed. It was already full of people, although Sunita couldn't see anyone famous.

"Right, sweetie," Rachel said to Sunita, giving her a big smile, "I'll take your friends to the set in a moment, but I'm afraid your mum and your gran will have to stay in here and watch the programme on TV."

Mrs Banerjee Senior sniffed at that, but Sunita was too excited to care.

"And these are the other finalists, Julia Simpson and Karl Holt," Rachel went on, ushering Sunita over to a corner where a teenage boy and girl were sitting with their families. "Look, darlings, this is Sunita Banerjee."

"Hi, Sunita, how're you doing?" Julia said. She was a short, plump girl with long brown hair and a nose-stud. Karl, who was tall and lanky, simply nodded at Sunita, looking too frightened to open his mouth.

"Hello," Sunita mumbled, suddenly realising something which hadn't hit her before. Both Julia and Karl were a lot older than she was.

"Super! I'll be back to talk to you again later." Rachel glanced at her watch. "Right, can everyone who's part of the studio audience come with me, please?"

"That's us!" Anya gasped. She flung her arms round Sunita and hugged her. "Good luck!"

"We probably won't get a chance to talk to you

till it's all over," Gemma said, "but we'll be cheering for you!"

"As loud as we can!" Carli added.

There wasn't much to do after the others had gone, and Sunita soon got bored. Her mum and her gran sat and chatted, but Sunita was too nervous to make conversation. It seemed like ages before Rachel came back again, and beckoned her, Julia and Karl over.

"It's only five minutes to transmission time now, so listen carefully and I'll tell you exactly what's going to happen." Rachel consulted her clipboard. "We'll have the introduction to the programme as usual, and then we've got Boyz playing live in the studio."

Sunita's eyes widened. Boyz playing live? They were a fantastic group, and Anya was totally in love with them!

"After Boyz there's a short cartoon, and that's when we'll get you and the judges onto the set. Rob from Boyz is one, along with Elena Moreno and Sophie Bennett from the soap *West Side*."

Sunita could hardly believe her ears. All the girls watched *West Side*, and Sophie Bennett was one of their favourite actresses.

"Kit will introduce the judges and then Eva will model the outfits. Obviously, Eva needs a few minutes to change into each one, so Kit will fill the time in-between by chatting to the judges, and to you."

Sunita was horrified, and Karl turned pale.

"You mean we have to *speak*?" he asked in a trembling voice.

"You won't have to say much," Rachel reassured him, quickly. "Kit will just ask you how you got the idea for your design, or something. Nothing to worry about."

Karl didn't look very convinced, and Sunita wasn't too happy either. She was sure that if she opened her mouth to speak, she'd be so terrified that nothing would come out.

"Don't look at the camera," Rachel advised them. "Just concentrate on Kit, and what he says to you, OK? Now, keep an eye on the TV, and I'll be back for you in about fifteen minutes."

"Are you all right, Sunny?" her gran asked anxiously. "Not feeling too nervous?"

"I'm fine *Dadima*," Sunita assured her, wishing it was true.

Live on Saturday was just about to start. The familiar theme tune blared out, and there were Kit and Eva, sitting on the sofa. Staring at the TV, Sunita found it hard to believe that in a very short time she'd be sitting on that familiar set, too.

"Hello to all you *Live on Saturday* fans!" shouted Kit. There was a quick shot of the audience clapping and cheering, and Sunita caught a brief glimpse of Anya and the others before the camera cut back to Kit. "Don't stay in bed – have fun, instead! And if there's anyone in your house who's still asleep, pour a bucket of cold water over them, that'll wake them up!"

"Good idea, Kit!" Eva replied. "Because if they don't get up now, they'll miss all the fab things we've got lined up for today's show. We've got Boyz playing live in the studio…"

As Kit and Eva continued to talk, Sunita suddenly became aware of two women who had walked into the Green Room together. She took a quick look over her shoulder, and immediately recognised Sophie Bennett from *West Side*, although the blonde actress looked much smaller than she appeared on-screen. Sunita was so thrilled, she couldn't help staring.

The other woman, tall and dark-haired, was less familiar, but Sunita was sure she'd seen her before, in a newspaper or a magazine. Then she realised. Of course! It had to be Elena Moreno, the fashion designer!

Not liking to stare for too long, Sunita turned back to the TV and watched Kit introduce Boyz.

"That sounds like Anya screaming her head off!" she muttered with a grin, as the audience began cheering and Boyz launched into their hit single, *Broken Heart*.

"Hello, Sophie, Elena! Super to see you both!" Rachel appeared halfway through the song, and beamed at the two judges. "Right, where are my competition finalists? Come along, sweeties, time to go."

"This is it!" Sunita told herself, taking a deep breath.

"Good luck, Sunny," said her mum, giving her a big hug.

"And whatever happens, remember we're *very* proud of you!" her gran added.

Sunita was trembling with nerves and excitement as Rachel led them all down the corridor, and into the *Live on Saturday* studio. At first Sunita was disappointed because the set looked so much smaller and more cramped than it did on TV, partly because there were so many bright lights and cameras and people moving around. The small audience were seated on the far side of the set, and Sunita could see Gemma, Carli and Anya waving at her. She waved back.

"This is Geoff, the Floor Manager," Rachel told them, as a young man with his hair in a ponytail

hurried towards them. "He'll get you all seated while the cartoon's on."

The Floor Manager quickly took Sunita, Karl, Julia and the two judges across the studio to the sofa. Kit Wilson was sitting there already, chatting to Rob Keeler, Boyz' lead singer. Sunita had seen both Kit and Rob on TV hundreds of times. Now here they both were, right next to her... She could hardly get her head round it.

Kit broke off his conversation to smile at them, and reached for his notes. "Hi! Nice to meet you all."

"Two minutes, Kit," called someone.

Sophie Bennett and Elena Moreno sat down on the big sofa with Kit and Rob, while Sunita and the others were given chairs. Sunita fidgeted nervously between Julia and Karl. She felt too hot under the studio lights, which were so bright she could hardly see anything at all. Please let this be over soon, she prayed silently. Oh, and please let me *win*...

"Great cartoon, that, hope you enjoyed it," Kit began. Sunita suddenly realised that they must be on air, and instantly she froze. "Now," he continued, "I'm sure you all remember that a while ago we launched our Young Fashion Designer of the Year competition. We'll be showing you the finalists' designs very shortly, but first let's meet the judges..."

Kit turned to Rob and started interviewing him, and Sunita relaxed slightly. She was intrigued to see that Kit's lines appeared on a screen in front of them, and that all he had to do was read them off. She'd thought that the presenters learnt their lines or made them up as they went along.

Having spoken to both Rob and Sophie, Kit turned to Elena. "It looks like a glamorous life being a fashion designer, Elena, but is there more to it than that?"

"Absolutely," Elena agreed with a smile. She looked very elegant in a simple, but beautifully-cut, black dress which Sunita longed to sketch. "But it's a very rewarding career for people with the right talent."

"And our finalists are certainly talented!" Kit commented. The camera homed in on them, and Sunita felt herself blush. "Let's make a start then. First we have fifteen-year-old Julia Simpson, from Manchester..."

Right on cue, Eva Jones appeared from behind the set, wearing the lime-green trouser suit which Julia had designed.

"What gave you the idea for this outfit, Julia?" Kit asked.

"Well, Eva seems to wear trousers on the show a

lot," Julia explained. "I thought this colour would suit her."

It *did*, Sunita thought rather enviously. The trouser-suit was very striking, and flattered the presenter's slim figure. Sunita decided gloomily that Julia had a very good chance of winning.

Kit turned to the judges to ask them briefly what they thought of Julia's design, and then it was time for the second outfit.

"Our next finalist is fourteen-year-old Karl Holt, from Norwich," Kit announced as Eva came out once more.

This time there was a gasp from the people on the set. Eva was wearing the long black evening dress Karl had designed. It was very full-skirted with layers of net, and made Eva look incredibly sophisticated. Sunita was sure now she had no chance of winning. Her design just wasn't as good as these two.

"So, Karl, what gave you the idea for this gorgeous dress?" Kit asked.

"I – er – " Karl was so scared he could hardly be heard. "I – um – just thought of it…"

Kit Wilson gave Karl a reassuring smile, and immediately turned to the judges.

"Sophie, what did you think of Karl's dress?"

Sunita tried to breathe deeply to calm herself as

Sophie responded. Her heart was beating so hard she thought she might faint if Kit Wilson didn't get to her soon.

"And now our third and final design from our youngest competitor," Kit said with a smile. "This is Sunita Banerjee's outfit. Sunita's ten, and comes from Duston…"

Sunita tried to smile as a camera was pointed in her direction, but she was sure she just looked as if she was pulling a terrible face. To her surprise, the audience gasped again as Eva came out in the cream suit. Then, a few of them started to applaud.

The outfit looked wonderful. Sunita was even surprised herself by how good it looked. The narrow trousers fitted Eva beautifully, and the tiny gold stars on the scarf glittered in the studio lights. Sunita had to sit on her hands because they were shaking so much. She'd never dreamt it would work so well.

"So, Sunita, how did you come up with the idea for that unusual design?" Kit asked her curiously.

"I – I got the idea from the kind of clothes my aunties and my cousins wear," Sunita stammered.

"Elena? What did you think of it?" Kit queried.

"Beautiful," Elena Moreno replied warmly, "I loved the combination of East and West. That's very fashionable at the moment."

113

Spotlight on Sunita

Sunita felt her heart swell with pride. She hoped Elena Moreno wasn't just being kind.

"Thanks, Eva, and thanks to all our finalists," Kit said. "And to give our judges a little time to make their decision, let's have a quick look at the video of Boyz' latest single, *You're In My Dreams*, out on Monday…"

Sunita stared hard at the judges as they huddled together on the sofa, talking in low voices. It was impossible to hear what they were saying, but every so often one of them glanced over at the finalists. Sunita caught Elena Moreno looking at her several times, and wondered if that was a good sign or not. Did she have *any* chance of winning?

"Right, we have a result!" Kit announced as the music video faded out. "First of all, let me thank our judges. They've had an incredibly difficult decision to make today…"

'Get a move on!' Sunita thought, impatiently.

"And the winner of the Young Fashion Designer of the Year Competition is…"

Sunita held her breath.

"Karl Holt!"

Sunita's face fell, but she clapped along with the rest of the people on the set as Karl, looking dazed, stood up, then sat down again, not quite sure what to do. Kit hurried over to shake his hand.

114

"Well done, Karl! You've won a fabulous computer and the chance to spend the day with Elena Moreno at her studio. And of course, all our finalists get their outfits to keep!"

"Congratulations," Sunita murmured to Karl, even though she was bitterly disappointed. Still, she told herself, it wasn't the end of the world, as the judges came over to shake hands with them and Eva came out wearing Karl's winning design again. After all, she'd done well to get to the final. She'd have to be content with that...

Sunita's gran was almost in tears in front of the TV in the Green Room. "Those judges need glasses!" she muttered darkly. "Sunita should have won!"

"Sunita's was the best!" Anya whispered to Gemma and Carli as they dutifully applauded along with the rest of the audience.

"Yeah, she should have won!" Gemma agreed.

"Poor Sunita. I hope she's not too disappointed," Carli said.

As another cartoon began, the Floor Manager

escorted Sunita and the others off the set and back to Rachel Nicholls.

"Bad luck, darlings," she said to Julia and Sunita. "If it makes you feel any better, the judges found it really, *really* hard to choose the winner."

Sunita forced a watery smile.

"You can go up to the gallery and watch the rest of the show if you like," Rachel went on. "And I'll get your outfits packed up so you can take them home with you."

"Sunita?" Sunita was surprised to hear her name as Rachel led the way over to the gallery. She turned round to find Elena Moreno smiling at her.

"Y-yes?" Sunita stammered, bewildered.

Elena drew her to one side. "Before I go, I just wanted to say how much I liked your design," she said in a low voice. "In fact, I liked it so much, I chose it as my winner. But the other two judges overruled me."

Sunita stared at her, unable to speak, hardly daring to believe her ears.

"Do you want to be a designer when you grow up?" Elena asked her.

Sunita nodded. "More than anything else!" she said passionately.

"Well, I think you've got a lot of talent." Elena shook Sunita by the hand as she turned to leave.

"So make sure you follow your dream and go for it!"

Sunita nodded again, too full of emotion to speak. A famous designer had told her she'd got talent! All of a sudden losing the competition didn't seem to matter at all.

Elena Moreno's words were echoing inside her head over and over again. *You've got a lot of talent...* She'd tell the others later, when she had the chance, but just for a little while, she could hug her special secret all to herself.

"Make sure you're quiet, because we don't want to frighten them," Gemma warned the others as she opened the door of the Gordons' shed. "Dad moved the hutch in here because it's warmer."

"Clever old Snowball!" Carli said as they all gathered quietly round the hutch and peeped in. The white rabbit was asleep in her nesting-box, tucked up warmly in the straw, with five tiny babies cuddled up against her.

"Ahh, they're so cute!" Sunita whispered.

"But they're *bald*!" Anya pointed out.

"Give them a chance, they were only born last night!" Gemma said. "They'll start growing some

Spotlight on Sunita

fur in three to four days. Then, Mum's friends from work can take them and give them good homes."

"We could call one 'Kit' and one 'Eva'," Anya suggested, eagerly. "Wasn't *Live on Saturday* brilliant? I want to be a TV presenter when I grow up!"

"I thought you wanted to be a fashion designer!" Lauren teased her.

Anya shook her head. "I'll leave that to Sunita – she's much better at it than I am!"

Sunita grinned. "Well, if Elena Moreno thinks I've got talent..."

The others groaned loudly.

"All right, all right!" Sunita laughed, "I know I've gone on and on about it! But I just want to say thanks for helping me get through all the problems I had with the competition. I couldn't have done it without you lot."

She held out her little fingers, and the girls linked themselves up into a circle.

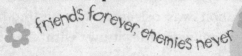

friends forever, enemies never

Sunita smiled, feeling warm despite the cold. She knew that, whatever happened, her best friends would always be there for her.

118

Girl TALK

Best Friends

1

Friends FOREVER

When Carli Pike joins Duston Middle School, she's in for a hard time. Alex Marshall, the notorious bully, is up to her old tricks again – she and her sidekicks are determined to turn the new girl's life into a nightmare.

It doesn't take the Best Friends long to see that Carli's in trouble, but Lauren loses interest and Anya is too wrapped up in her flash friend Astrid. Can Gemma and Sunita find the proof they need to help Carli survive Duston?

OH BROTHER!

The half-term break has finally arrived. Anya plans to shop till she drops! Gemma's chuffed because she's been allowed to get another pet rabbit. Lauren just can't wait to play loads of football.

But the others are seriously depressed. Sunita's gran is threatening to organise a private tutor and no one can get a word out of Carli. The holiday gets even worse when Anya's half-brother Christopher arrives. Will the Best Friends manage to hold together?

A Challenge for
LAUREN

Lauren goes pool crazy when she's selected as team captain for the annual swimming gala. But any celebrations are cut short when troublemaker Alex Marshall sets out to steal her place.

All the others would like to help, but are never around at the right time. Gemma, Carli and Sunita land in trouble when a helping hand turns sour and Anya's swamped by unwanted clothes! Will the Best Friends be there when Lauren needs them most?

More brilliant Best Friends books available from BBC Worldwide Ltd

The prices shown below were correct at the time of going to press. However BBC Worldwide Ltd reserve the right to show new retail prices on covers which may differ from those previously advertised in the text or elsewhere.

1 Friends Forever Gill Smith
0 563 38092 6 £2.99

2 Oh Brother! Narinder Dhami
0 563 38093 4 £2.99

3 Spotlight on Sunita Narinder Dhami
0 563 40552 X £2.99

4 A Challenge for Lauren Heather Maisner
0 563 40553 8 £2.99

All BBC titles are available by post from:
Book Service By Post,
PO Box 29, Douglas, Isle of Man, IM99 1BQ

Credit cards accepted.
Please telephone 01624 675137 or fax 01624 670923.
Internet http://www.bookpost.co.uk
or e-mail: bookshop@enterprise.net for details.

Free postage and packaging in the UK. Overseas customers: allow £1 per book (paperback) and £3 per book (hardback).